MOSLEY BY MOONLIGHT

Mosley by Moonlight

JOHN GREENWOOD

Walker and Company
New York

Copyright © 1984 by John Greenwood

First published in the United States of America
in 1985 by the Walker Publishing Company, Inc.

Library of Congress Cataloging in Publication Data

Hilton, John Buxton.
  Mosley by moonlight.

  I. Title.
PR6058.I5M6 1985   823'.914   84-17214
ISBN 0-8027-5606-9

Printed in the United States of America

10 9 8 7 6 5 4 3 2

1

Mosley laid out on his bedside table all that a man could need for a night's repose: his clasp-knife, his dented tin of black shag, his matches, his notebook and his leaking pre-war fountain pen. He hung his clothes over the chair, pulled the lap of his grey shirt as far over his knees as it would reach, slithered between the cold pub sheets and switched off the light. Five minutes later he switched it on again, scraped out his pipe, charged it and began to write.

Events in Hadley Dale had turned his mind at once to Lottie Pearson. They would have done, even without the revelations of Percy Allnut, *Chymist*. It had never been far from the top of his mind that one day Lottie Pearson, through no intention of her own, was going to disturb the peace of Hadley Dale. He had felt even more concerned since she had shacked up with Matthew Longden. That, he believed, was the contemporary phrase. Lottie Pearson would probably never have heard it, and Matthew Longden would certainly not use it if he had.

Percy Allnut, *Chymist* (he still had the archaic spelling in marbled lettering over his shop-front) had beckoned him in, the last market day he had been in Bradburn: a pair of knowingly suspicious eyes peeping between the Latin-labelled bottles of his window display. Percy sadly missed the day when his job had been to mix ingredients to the quantities prescribed. Now it was all brand names and trade leaflets. But his machines for pressing cachets and rolling pills, his cork-borers and suppository-moulds still lay handy on his bench – either in memory or as a symbol of hope.

Secretive and elliptical in speech, old Percy missed out whole stages in his arguments, but expected his listeners to stay with him, which they might have done if he had reached his conclusions by the same logic as other men. Mosley always did his best to follow Percy. His conclusions were often worth hearing, however he had come by them. Today he showed Mosley a half-inch of greyish sludge in the bottom of a glass beaker.

'Porridge.'

It was safest not to comment too early.

'Arsenic,' old Allnut added, his head nodding. 'Reads too many books. Always did. Used to have four or five a week from the library when he lived in Bradburn. These writers are always slipping arsenic into people's porridge. Wouldn't work, you know. Too gritty. They'd notice.'

Percy stopped talking, and for a moment Mosley faced the possibility that this was all.

'Whose porridge?' he asked, after a long enough silence.

'Matthew Longden's lady-friend's,' Percy said. 'Brought it in this time last week for me to analyse. Very discreet. Not a word to a soul. Nods, winks, blind horses.'

'And you found arsenic?'

Allnut reached for a test-tube containing something cloudy in suspension.

'Sand. Very peculiar, you know. Last time, it was the other way round. Not Scarborough sand. Not Blackpool. Egg-timer, I'd say. Fine stuff. Take the enamel off your teeth. Just about the right amount for the average egg-timer. And I ask you – why should history repeat itself – backwards?'

They both knew what he was talking about: Matthew Longden's first wife – well, his wife. He had never divorced her and, of course, had never been married to Lottie Pearson. His wife had put sand in his porridge. That was what had been assumed when he had brought a sample to be analysed by Percy Allnut. And Percy had tipped Mosley off, just as he had now. As was to be expected, no complaint had been put in. Matthew Longden was unaware that Mosley knew about it.

'Mind you,' Percy said funereally, 'when a man takes up with a foreign woman twenty years younger than himself, we must expect to find sand in somebody's porridge.'

The Assistant Chief Constable and Detective-Superintendent

Thomas Grimshaw sat separately by their private hearths watching the early-evening television. The news of the day was unfolded: an armed conflict in Old Testament country and a parliamentary by-election reported on the dramatic lines originally developed by football commentators. During the ensuing magazine programme, the two men became traumatically attentive. Not only was one of their own uniformed constables being interviewed, but it was PC Joseph Ormerod, whom it was firm policy not to parade in the public view more than was avoidable. It was for this reason that Ormerod was stationed in a remote village in the very area where Mosley was the reigning genius and where, except for the oversight of compulsory sheep-dipping, it could be assumed that he would seldom have anything to do. Joe Ormerod, a burly, slow-moving, slow-speaking man in his late twenties, had a brow which sloped backwards like that of a certain species of ape, and which was almost totally obscured by a frieze of black eyebrows. It was this face that now looked out from their screens at Superintendent Grimshaw and the Assistant Chief Constable. Ormerod's fierce concentration seemed to banish from his eyes any grain of intelligence that loyal friends might have claimed to discern there in his brighter moments.

'Well, aye,' he was saying, with an uncharacteristic leaning towards enthusiasm. 'I'd have said in my opinion, personally, meself, that it had one eye on a luminous stalk, about four feet long, waving about in front of it. Only it was not growing out of its head, where you'd expect a thing to have an eye on a stalk. It was growing out of where its chin would have been, if it had had a chin.'

This was an extraordinarily long statement for Joe Ormerod to undertake. Tom Grimshaw guessed he was reading from a teleprompter, which might account for his expression of tortured application.

'It was about half as big again as an ordinary human, and it had big feet – big, webbed, feet, like a frogman's flippers.'

'Did it speak to you?' the interviewer asked: Ellerman Tovey, a longstanding non-friend of the county force.

'A few words.'

'What were they?'

3

'I don't know. I couldn't cotton on to the language.'

'And you weren't afraid of this thing?'

'I saw no cause to be. It had the look – well, it looked as if it had just been out rabbiting.'

'Is it normal for creatures half as big again as an ordinary human, and with eyes on stalks, to go rabbiting in Hadley Dale?'

'It's a situation I've not come across before,' Omerod said.

'And what have your superiors had to say about this?'

'I haven't reported it yet,' Ormerod said. 'To tell you the truth, I'm not sure that any offence has been committed, as far as the law of the land is concerned.'

UFOs had not previously disturbed the peace of this shoulder of the hills. Then, a couple of nights ago, men returning home from rural hostelries had reported a luminous crystal dome in the middle distance.

'You don't think, for example,' Ellerman Tovey was saying, 'that this might have been a fancy-dress cover-up for something like illegal immigration or drug traffic?'

'We get very little of that sort of thing up Hadley Dale,' Joe Ormerod informed the viewing public. The Assistant Chief Constable's face bore an expression that impelled his wife to bring him an unsolicited whisky and soda.

Hadley Dale consisted of some thirty-six square miles of uncultivated fell and intake farmland. Bits of it that had once been in Lancashire were now in Yorkshire; and other bits vice versa. Commissions had redrawn boundaries and fuelled hostilities that the history-books said had come to an end in 1485. Hadley Dale was part of the vast, largely sterile tract for which Detective-Inspector Mosley was answerable. According to the latest census, it accommodated 503 of Her Majesty's subjects, who did not constitute one of the Chief Constable's major headaches. Should they ever constitute a minor one, it would undoubtedly suffice to farm the problem out to Mosley, in whose hands such things had a habit of vaporizing out of human knowledge. Mosley appeared to know every one of these 500-odd characters by their Christian names and had never been known to haul one of them out of the Dale for formal correction.

Few would have called the men of the Dale imaginative but there was a poker-faced exaggeration in their run-of-the-mill story-telling. There was, for example, old Tom Appleyard's yarn about reaching out with the crook of his stick for a field mushroom so well-developed that he found a sheep sheltering beneath it. There was Brad Oldroyd, returning home from the Plough through the private cemetery of the now derelict manor of Thurstock, who had seen not one, but forty-nine ghosts sitting on the edges of open graves. He had assured himself by counting their heads twice, in the archaic cardinals used in the neighbourhood for the numbering of flocks: *eena, deena, pithera, pimp* –

Beneath their dour exteriors, Mosley's people, with the possible exception of Joseph Ormerod, were a sensitive race, their lives constantly in fee to such imponderables as whether the changes in the county border might affect the climate. The unpunctuality of brewers' deliveries also occasionally worried them. And they were somewhat remote from the real world, since they lived in the marginal reception area of several TV networks, which flickered across their screens in a jazzy haze. It seemed improbable that their inventiveness would extend to intergalactic scouts, yet here was PC Ormerod, casually assuming that Martians, Venusians, Betelgeusians, Alpha Centaurians or whatever had come here simply to trespass in search of conies. And since he saw no way of bringing them into a court of law, he had not considered them worth reporting.

Inspector Mosley was therefore sought, and, due to some atypical unpreparedness on his part, was located within less than half a day. He was ordered to go at once to Hadley Dale to scotch all rumours, and to prevent once and for all the fermentation of any myth or legend. Above all, he was to get hold of Joseph Ormerod – not in order to talk sense into him, for the ACC took a pragmatic view of mortal limitations – but to remind him in memorable terms of standing orders with respect to statements to the media.

The evening after Mosley's mission, the Superintendent and ACC were again sitting hypnotized by their tubes at a few minutes after six o'clock. The regional newscast opened harmlessly enough. This time, the cameras were out in the field, on a relative plateau amid the slopes of Hadley Dale, panning in on six marks in the grass which might conceivably have been made by the landing-gear of a circular object some ninety feet in circumference. So far, innocuous enough: the furrows could have been made by almost anything. But the shock was still to come. A lecturer from Bradcaster Poly was called on to draw comparisons with other sightings of UFOs. The ACC snorted at his wife, and Superintendent Grimshaw laughed hollowly. A few seconds later, both men were sitting forward on the edges of their chairs.

For the next expert witness was none other than Mosley. Mosley was being interviewed in the open air, standing by a broken gate between limestone walls: Mosley with his black homburg clamped absurdly straight on his head; Mosley with his buttonless raincoat flapping open to reveal his shiny blue suit and disreputable woollen cardigan. Mosley's eyes, singularly sapped of life, were gazing inanely into the wrong camera.

It was true to say – though they would not have conceded the point without reservations – that Grimshaw and the ACC set a certain value on Mosley. In his weatherbeaten bailiwick he was an accepted figure, though those who accepted him might not all be representative of the latter decades of this century. But the Force had to consider its prestige, and it did not care to advertise Mosley gratuitously outside his own proper corner.

'I'd be grateful, Inspector Mosley, if you would tell viewers what you were telling me just now.'

The ACC had tightened his grip on the arms of his chair. It was like seeing the approach of a dentist who is making a bad job of hiding the forceps in the palm of his hand. Mosley was staring into some tens of thousands of north-country living-rooms like a man taken unawares by the incomprehensible.

'You actually encountered one of these creatures?'

Mosley found his tongue.

'That is correct.'

'My God!' Tom Grimshaw said. 'Did you see that jerky shift in the close-up? They've chopped this all over the place. God knows what Mosley actually said – but even God doesn't know what the cutting-room will have made of it. Tovey's turned this into a farce.'

Mosley was goggling out of the screen like an imbecile. Ellerman Tovey helped him out in his kindliest kindergarten manner.

'Could you describe him for us?'

'He stood about seven foot three inches tall,' Mosley said.

With an eye on a stalk?'

'Five eyes,' Mosley said. 'On five stalks. Growing up out of the back of his neck. They came up and over the back of his head.'

The ACC got out of his chair and began to pace up and down. In another, slightly less sought-after suburb of the same city, Tom Grimshaw was holding his breath.

'And have you been able to form any theories, Mr Mosley?'

'It seems obvious to me –' Mosley was rattled – and he had never been an easy man to rattle – 'it seems obvious to me that he had been left behind by the main body.'

'You mean, he'd missed his saucer?'

'He'd missed whatever he came by.'

'And I understand you actually spoke to the creature?'

'The creature spoke to me,' Mosley said, not without truculence.

'You had no difficulty in understanding him?'

'Of course not.'

'And what did he say to you?'

'He wanted to know where was the nearest pub that's in the *Real Ale Guide*.'

Cut to 'Nationwide'. Sue Lawley was sitting in the studio with a young man at a table loaded with dates. He was trying to get into the *Guinness Book of Records* for a stone-spitting marathon. Superintendent Grimshaw was already halfway across the room. He knew the phone was going to ring.

'Does that bloody idiot,' the ACC wanted to know, 'really think that extra-terrestrial beings come charging across several million light-years, having attended WEA classes in English, and with their CAMRA subscriptions paid up?'

'I'm afraid Mosley was out of his depth,' Grimshaw attempted.

'Depth? Depth? Mosley hasn't got a depth. His Plimsoll line is round his ankles. He's only got to step in a puddle and he'll

7

capsize. I want him in front of my desk at nine sharp in the morning, Tom.'

'That might not be too easy,' Grimshaw said, he hoped persuasively. It was rare for him to side openly with Mosley, for fear of becoming too closely identified with him. But he had some sympathy with the way Mosley had fallen victim to Tovey.

'It had better be more than easy,' the ACC said. 'Nine sharp.'

'I'll try. But I have a feeling that Mosley's going to be more than usually difficult to run to earth for a week or two.'

'I expect the silly bugger will be up all night waiting to get away on the next saucer.'

2

Mosley was aware that he had done badly, but had no way of knowing yet how badly. He knew that he had allowed himself to be overawed by technology. He did not realize how ruthlessly he was going to be edited, but he did know that the thing had been all over before he had said what he wanted to. He knew as well as the next man that this had nothing to do with astral reconnaissance. Even after half an hour of the Pennine wind on his cheeks, he still felt unsettled. It was rare for Mosley to be unsettled. He spent most of his time settling other people.

Mosley was normally as integral a part of his environment as any tree, chimney-cowl or drystone wall. Now everything his eye lit upon seemed somehow alien. He had let his environment down at a time when it was under threat. He was under no illusion about these characters who had come to Hadley Dale. They brought disruption to the quiet, resigned lives that Mosley's people wanted to be allowed to get on with. They had come up and shot their film on Matthew Longden's land. If there'd been any trouble up there, Lottie Pearson would be at the hub of it. Lottie Pearson was trouble-prone. In the next few days he was going to have to be unusually mobile. He was going to listen unseen and watch unheard in places a long way apart. And this brought him up squarely against his never-vanishing problem of getting about. Now into his fifties, he was beginning to feel long in the tooth for the transport war that he had been waging for years with the Force.

In principle and on paper, he was entitled to a car. In practice, his was always the vehicle that was borrowed or seconded, its gaskets blown by drivers he barely knew by name.

'Think of how much more you can see,' Tom Grimshaw once told him, 'when you do your rounds on foot. And I'll see that you never miss out on boot allowance.'

When he was a young policeman, an old policeman had given Mosley two pieces of advice. One was to contrive to be taken for a bit of fool: information came more readily to your ears if people did not think you mattered. The second principle was never to hurry to a job: give yourself time to see things on the way.

Grimshaw spent much time in last-ditch exasperation with Mosley, but knew that he was not a fool. The Assistant Chief Constable remained open-minded. Over the years, Mosley had covered prodigious distances by the use of his limbs, knowing by heart the ever-diminishing bus and train time-tables, occasionally covering urgent stretches on a bicycle. Sometimes he cadged lifts – in private cars, on farm lorries, milk-floats and tractor-drawn trailers; once, memorably, on a steam-roller. There were hundreds of drivers in Mosley's part of the world whose feet went to clutch and brake at the sight ahead of them of the stubby little figure in homburg and flapping raincoat.

But this afternoon nothing and no one seemed to be going his way up Hadley Dale. Only up the last stretch, the punishing gradient past the ruins of Thurstock Manor, did he ride amid a load of returning milk-churns. He knew that he would hear something unique in the Plough this evening. Tonight, the communal imagination of the Plough would have had something to set it going. It would have been here in the Plough that the inter-stellar raiding-party would have broken off for lunch.

And it proved to be so. While management had gone down to

the *Good Food Guide* recommendation in Bradburn, the rank and file, with eye-stalks where their chins ought to have been, had consumed the landlord's entire stock of Wensleydale. The eight-footer who had alarmed Joe Ormerod had parked his stilts in the porch and shown himself a dab hand at darts, his stalk oscillating off-puttingly as he took aim.

'Saw you on the telly, Mr Mosley. Have you started charging for autographs?'

'You'll be getting an autograph on the bottom of a summons, if I see anybody else riding on your crossbar.'

He was in no mood for banter, but there was no way of staying out of it.

'By God, they could shift some ale, that lot could.'

'Women pinting it, too.'

'Pinting ale – and the rest. Arthur says it's the first time he's ever had that Pimm's bottle down off the shelf.'

'It was Lottie Pearson who asked for that.'

Mosley edged closer.

'What was Lottie Pearson doing in here?'

'Oh, they did some scenes up round the big house, you know, and somebody must have spotted her talent. She had what they called a walking-on part – well, a bit more than walking-on, the way it worked out. Then at the end of the morning, they all came down here. They had a drink or two, then Lottie went down to town with the nobs. I reckon they went to that new-fangled Tudor place.'

'And what had Matthew Longden to say about that?'

'Do you know, I haven't set eyes on him since?'

'Nor Lottie Pearson either. Funny, that. She makes an excuse to come down the street most days, as a rule.'

'Some of the hangers-on seemed to think the world belonged to them. In and out of Toby Warhurst's hen-house as if it was a free-for-all.'

'Broken down a length of Billy Halliday's fencing with their cable.'

'Two lambs chased, over on Bundock's. One of the producers had a dog that had been yapping in the back of his car all the morning. Straight up the hillside when he let it out.'

Mosley fought to memorize details: he never liked producing

a notebook in a public bar. He'd have to corner one or two and ask the sort of question they didn't like answering. He asked for a room for the night. Then Joe Ormerod came in, his backward-sloping, beetle-browed forehead beamed in on the beer-pumps like the warhead of a rocket.

'Had you for a bit of a sucker, didn't they, Joe? Saying you couldn't understand the language? The man was only a Geordie.'

Ormerod scowled in a manner that would have had strangers looking for cover.

'You'll not have found any more Daleks out rabbiting, then, Joe?'

'That's not what I meant,' Ormerod said. Mosley did not join in. If they had made a monkey out of Joe, they had not done too badly out of John Miller Mosley, either. It was merciful that this company knew how to shift subjects at a tangent.

'They'd no flies on those bull-frog costumes, you know. Had to strip right down when they wanted a pee.'

'It's all right laughing,' Ormerod said. 'They did a lot of damage. One of their vans backed into Isaac Oldman's gatepost, snapped it clean off at ground-level.'

'Aye. And they say that post's stood there since Saxon times.'

'I'd better have a word with Isaac,' Mosley said.

It all needed to be recorded, which was why Mosley, not five minutes in bed, stretched out his hand to put on his light again. It was never safe to leave note-taking till the morning. And contrary to all forms and forecasts, he was in the office the next day before either the Assistant Chief Constable or Grimshaw. When the two senior statesmen came in, Mosley was sitting at his trestle-table, his hat upside down beside a pile of reports to which his pen was just putting the finishing touches. He had not taken off his coat, and the general impression he gave was of a man who intended to be away to his hills the moment he had scratched out a couple more syllables.

But it was there that any resemblance ended to a man of pristine vigour. Mosley had slept badly. His eyes were blood-shot and hazed. His razor had missed bristles. The ACC – in full dress uniform, for some reason that only his desk-diary knew about – exchanged head-jerks with Grimshaw. And

Grimshaw, laying his hand on Mosley's shoulder in a manner meant to be encouraging, ushered the inspector into the sanctum.

'Why the hell didn't you make it clear, Mosley, that you knew this was only a television commercial they were making?'

As a rule, Mosley listened to rebukes from the ACC in a silence that might be taken as contrite, if the ACC cared so to interpret it. He seldom uttered an argument in self-justification: simply waited until the spate of words was spent, then shuffled off about his next interest as if nothing had been said. Today he surprised even himself by the words that came out of him.

'What else could it have bloody well been?'

The ACC digested this. He was not a man who had ever imagined himself tolerating insolence. Now that it had happened, he could think of no immediate thing that it was safe to do about it.

'A pity you couldn't have used that tone to Ellerman Tovey.'

'I know I was on the slow side,' Mosley said. 'I thought it was only a trial run. They'd finished before I knew they'd started.'

'Has the mob departed?'

'Yes, sir. They were only up there three days.'

'What the hell do they hope to advertise by landing Martians in Hadley Dale?'

'After-shave lotion.'

'I don't see the connection.'

'Half each advertisement shows people who don't need after-shave. Martians don't, because they have eyes where their chins ought to be.'

The ACC looked at Mosley through narrowing eyes.

'Are you trying to take the piss out of me, Mosley?'

'That's how it was. Some of the village women were shown cuddling them, stroking their chins.'

Including Lottie Pearson. One could hope that Matthew Longden did not know. But Mosley said nothing about this angle.

'I'm not looking forward to the next few days up in Hadley,' he said.

'Then stay away from the damned place. Go somewhere where there's some danger you might find something to do.'

'That'll be Hadley Dale, sir, Thursday afternoon.'

'Why Thursday afternoon?'

'Early closing in Bradburn. People flocking up to Hadley.'

'I don't see why they should. Everybody knows Martians *haven't* landed.'

'With respect, sir – everybody doesn't know that. There's always somebody who only half hears any story. People will be going up there for picnics. We shall have lost property, litter, walls broken down, wild flowers dug up by the roots. Last Spring Holiday, the viper's bugloss was stripped completely from Wellman's Bank.'

'These are hardly matters of top priority for a criminal investigation department.'

The ACC took slow, deep breaths. He seemed to be exercising no guidance over the confrontation at all.

'I hold you responsible for seeing that there's no trouble of any kind, Mosley.'

And in the outer office, Grimshaw had picked up Mosley's small stack of reports.

'I take it these were destined to reach me eventually. How long is it since you last brought a charge against anyone, Mosley?'

'Late last year. Unlawful possession of unstable gelignite.'

'I can see that even you could hardly overlook that. Now we suddenly get this lot. Quite a day for brainstorms, yesterday. And are you hoping to get clearance to travel down to Kent to pursue some of these?'

'I can see there could be objections to that.'

'Why Kent, all of a sudden? What have you suddenly got against the garden of England?'

'They've moved down there to make their next film.'

'The hordes of Venus moving in where Hitler recoiled?'

'They are going to shoot a sequence of *King Lear* on Dover cliffs.'

'What's that in aid of?'

'After-shave lotion. King Lear didn't need it. They're going to show his beard blowing about in a Channel gale.'

'We might, Mosley, ask Kent to take these things up for us. To try to find a cameraman who stole four eggs, value twenty pence. Critical damage done to a brass bedstead, temporarily in use as a fencing-length, valued at ninety-five pence. That isn't *criminal* damage.'

'The farmer had asked the engineer to desist.'

'Failure to stop and report damage to a Saxon gatepost, valued at forty pence. Who has a Saxon gatepost in Hadley Dale?'

'*Had* one, sir. Isaac Oldham.'

'And where does he think he'll get another for forty pence? Or was that the Saxon valuation? Is that what he'd got it insured for? This is going to add astronomical digits to our retrieval statistics, Mosley. It comes to over one pound fifty on the first three cases alone.'

'There's also the question of the producer's dog. Protection of Livestock Act, 1953. It doesn't pay to drag our feet over that kind of thing, up in my part of the world.'

'You don't state that any animal was killed or even injured.'

'Two lambs very frightened. Two witnesses. Chased in such a way as might reasonably be expected to cause suffering within the meaning of the Act.'

Something came into Mosley's tone that was akin to his explosion in front of the ACC.

'How can we expect people to behave if we ignore the first complaint they've made for thirty years?'

'I'll have a word with the Assistant Chief. But I wouldn't be too optimistic, if I were you.'

Mosley screwed up his pen and made ready for Hadley Dale.

Lottie Pearson. Matthew Longden. Sand in Lottie's porridge. Out of an egg-timer. A few years ago there had been sand in Matthew's porridge. Mosley had better make sure that all parties understood each other. Better still, he'd cast a quiet eye over them first. Tomorrow morning, Bradburn market.

Matthew Longden and Lottie Pearson were one of the market-day features of Bradburn, a sight less charitably interpreted by those who knew them than by the increasing number who didn't. There was something striking about them. Casual observers found their companionship touching.

Matthew Longden was an elderly man, not far short of seventy, though older in appearance than his birth-certificate attested. He suffered from a medicine-defying strain of osteo-arthritis. But though he was a cripple, he always managed to keep himself going – with Lottie Pearson's help. He moved unhurriedly, suggesting dignity rather than pain. He was from all aspects a dignified man. He had dignified forbears. In his working years he had followed the dignified profession of accountancy. The more dignified stratum of Bradburn's mer-chants would trust no one else with their books. When he had been forced to retire, and had moved up to Hadley Dale, a year before his wife left him, the removal van had climbed the hills with dignity. The village had been impressed. He did not merely exude dignity – he appeared to confer it on others.

The woman who came shopping with him was twenty years his junior. She was well-built and German, with something about her bearing that suggested she had been pretty in youth. She was robust and becoming chubby, though without any hint – yet – of negligent obesity. Her ampleness was of the kind that gives German men pride, satisfying them that they are feeding their women properly. She had greying hair that still showed streaks of its Gretchen-like origins, and which arranged itself in natural waves. She had a shining country complexion and, it seemed, a boundless vivacity. She was a woman who would not acknowledge that any fellow-human was a stranger. She talked to all and sundry, refusing to differentiate divisions of class or any other supposed distinguishing qualities. For some people that she waylaid, this could be a weird experience, for, although she could speak in rapid English on any subject that presented itself, there were strict limits to the range of the language that she had learned – or ever intended to learn. Her command of idiom was not infrequently quaint, and whenever she was defeated by vocabulary, she simply inserted a word from her native tongue, irrespective of the linguistic capacity of her hearers. Once, for example, in a supermarket, she gave an unsolicited cookery lesson to the file of housewives at the check-out, urging them to make their husbands a bodisome German pudding based largely on cornflower, which she called *Gries*. And, since the dish appeared to consist of *grease* in extraordinary quantity, there were doubts about her sanity.

But she was an ideal comrade in the High Street for an almost completely immobilized Matthew Longden. Together they had developed the minutiae of co-operation needed for the weekly household shopping.

They always parked on a waste space behind the Congregational Chapel, and, while Matthew Longden was switching off the engine, turning off the car-heater and pulling up the handbrake an extra notch, Lottie Pearson was going to the boot for her shopping-bags and his walking-stick, arriving at the door in the nick of time to help his left ankle over the sill without drawing undue public attention to his disability. They then walked together, she guiding him by the arm above the elbow, along the alley which led behind the backs of the shops into Cross Street – a perfect combination of *adagio* and suppressed *brio*.

Those who did not know them even wondered if they were father and daughter – or, more probably, a niece out with a favourite uncle. There was a fresher, more spontaneous glitter of friendship between them than is common between separated generations who are compelled to live together.

Matthew Longden and Lottie Pearson were not related to each other. Nor were they married. There was something slightly strange about that. It was now all of eight years since Betty Longden had deserted her husband. He could have freed himself from her as a simple matter of form, and Lottie Pearson could equally easily have got rid of her current legal spouse. Yet there seemed no signs that either of them wanted to put their relationship on a more orthodox footing. Not that that mattered from any material standpoint. Matthew Longden had made properly attested provision for Lottie and no one believed that it would not be a generous one. The hill-folk knew of many a common-law partnership that had outlasted blessed and sealed unions. Matthew Longden had talked to Mosley about it once, though it was none of Mosley's business. Clearly he had wanted a man of Mosley's standing to know that his mistress had nothing to complain about. There were no other contenders for his property, and if she chose not to remain with him for the rest of her days, she would still not be meanly treated. The line that Matthew Longden took – or said that he took – was that as she was not tied to him by marriage, her freedom was assured. Smiling wryly, he told Mosley that if he wanted to keep her, he had to behave himself; but if she found that she had been mistaken about him, she would not find herself locked in.

Every Friday morning they visited the shops in an order that never changed. In Teape's Lottie took her voluble turn at the bacon counter, while Matthew edged his way towards the cheeses. Then Lottie wanted bits and pieces of haberdashery and Matthew needed tobacco and pipe-cleaners. They went to the library together, they both knew what they were looking for in the supermarket. And if they were temporarily parted at any stage, they came upon each other again with smiles that might have signalled the end of a long lovers' parting – Matthew's always tinged with a hint of sad gratitude, while Lottie scintillated with controlled geniality. Finally they would go to the Black Boy, Matthew for a pint of mild and bitter, and Lottie for whatever she fancied, usually a bottle of one of the sweeter brews of stout. After this she would go alone to the Congregational vestry, which was turned into a rudimentary coffee-bar on market days. There Mrs Pearson Senior would be sitting with a cup of tea.

Mrs Pearson was the mother of the second English husband from whom Lottie had been lucky to escape. She also lived in Hadley Dale, but was a woman of ill-tempered independence who always came down by bus, refusing a lift in the car. She would, she said, have missed the company of the other passengers.

Lottie always went across for a chat with her before going back to the Black Boy for Matthew. And she always took the old woman's heavier items of shopping home for her in the boot. This was a physical convenience so invaluable that even Sarah Pearson had not the bad grace to refuse it.

On this particular Friday morning Mosley was standing at the corner of Cornmarket Street and Tinker's Lane in time to see Matthew Longden's old blue Austin Cambridge come into town at the lower end of the Ribblesdale Road. His first impression was that Longden was alone in the front seat, but at the worst of moments a furniture van moved from rest and obscured his view. He had to wait until the car was turning into the Chapel yard before he could confirm that Matthew had indeed come into town on his own. It was the first time Mosley had known that to happen since Lottie Pearson had moved in as his housekeeper.

He sheltered in a shop doorway towards the less commercial end of Water Street. Whichever route Longden intended to follow, he would be certain not to come down here. Mosley watched the old man's painful progress as he forced himself with determination towards Teape's.

Mosley made his way to the Chapel, where instant coffee was being served by a knot of worthy women. He spotted Mrs Pearson sitting alone. He had known her for most of his life and recognized her as a type that had still not disappeared from the remoter areas of the north country. She seemed to regard it as a matter for personal shame if ever she showed herself suscepti-ble to any of the nobler emotions – especially love, pity or a capacity for self-sacrifice (which she had been practising all her life). Lottie had lived with Sarah Pearson throughout her second marriage, and, when Sarah's son had left the two of them, she had remained there, to the accompaniment of one long strident quarrel that filled all their waking minutes. Perhaps the common ground between them had been their opinion of Jack Pearson.

Mosley moved towards the old woman in the tea-room, and she spotted him when he was halfway across the room.

'I think I'll draw up and take a cup with you,' he said.

'Aye. Take that chair.'

'So how are you keeping, Mrs Pearson?'

'I mustn't grumble.'

'Been having fun and games up the Dale, then?'

She did not seem to know immediately what he meant.

'Oh, that!' she said, when the television crew occurred to her. 'And there's some that ought to have known better than get mixed up in it. I don't know what Mr Longden would have to say about that, I'm sure.'

It was not simply that Sarah Pearson disapproved of acting and cameras. Innovations and publicity in general offended her. It was tempting to believe that she disapproved of everything – and certainly of her daughter-in-law's liaison with the big house. She must surely scorn Matthew Longden's morals. She hated him like a mortal enemy of her sort. But she would even pretend to respect him, if that was another lash for Lottie's back.

'So Lottie got mixed up in the acting?'

'You can ask her yourself. She'll be along in a minute.'

So Sarah Pearson did not know yet that Lottie had not come to Bradburn this morning? Hadley House was beyond the outskirts of the village. What went on up there could be very private. Mosley looked at the old woman's two shopping-bags. They were very full. She had bought a stone of potatoes as well as her usual groceries. She must have made two visits to the vestry to get it all here. It was going to be a struggle for her to get this lot to the bus. He had better tell her.

'I see Matthew's come to town on his own this morning.'

'I'm not surprised. I'm surprised he wants anything to do with her at all, after the exhibition she made of herself. Letting those creatures put their arms round her, stroking their chins. Letting them maul her about – then going off in the car with them.'

'You'd better let me give you a hand with your parcels.'

'I can manage.'

And maybe she would have tried, even if she had collapsed in the street. Up in the Dale, they looked on it as a hallmark of character, to push stubbornness to the extreme of stupidity. You had to ignore what the likes of Sarah Pearson said, and do what had to be done. Mosley stayed talking to her till he saw that she was getting worried about the time. Then he picked

19

up her bags, and carried them down to the bus station ahead of her.

After that, he pushed his footsteps along to the quieter end of Fullergate, where he ran into Brad Oldroyd, who had been having a saw set at Hebblewhite's.

'Nah, Brad.'

'Nah, Jack.'

'Settled down up yonder, has it now, then?'

'Aye – but it's funny where things will lead folk.'

Meaning something about Lottie Pearson? For Mosley at the moment, all roads led to Lottie Pearson. But this was something different.

'Rum do,' Oldroyd said. 'Three chaps up there today, looking at marks in the grass where that flying tea-caddy's supposed to have come down. Had surveyors' instruments with them, drawing-boards, the bloody lot.'

'Highways Department?'

'Chaps from away.'

'Funny, you know,' Mosley said. 'There's always somebody, somewhere, who only hears half of any story that's going. I was saying in our office –'

'I thought it was only you and Joe Ormerod got took in like that.'

Then he caught the look in Mosley's eyes.

'Sorry, Jack.'

'Brad, were you down in the village when that lot were swarming the street?'

'Yes. Some bugger had boxed me in with his car.'

'Lottie Pearson was getting up to some larks, so they tell me.'

'Oh, aye. She let herself go good and proper with one of those doodle-buggers. Like a couple of kids up Sandy Lane, they were.'

Mosley waited to be told why she had not come to town with her lord and master this morning. Oldroyd did not mention the fact – which could only mean that he did not know about it. But he knew something else.

'Funny thing about Lottie Pearson. Ted Hunter told me. He does odd jobs up there, you know, now the old fellow isn't so good in the garden. Lottie went one morning to get the car out, found the wheel-nuts slackened off on all four. Called Ted to tighten them up for her.'

'Since the spacemen?'

'Couple of weeks before that.'

The same vintage as the sand in the porridge, then.

'How did she know they were loose?' Mosley asked. 'You'd hardly expect a woman to check on that every time.'

'Whoever had done it had been interrupted. The hub-caps were still off and lying there.'

'They didn't report it.'

'No. She told Ted Hunter to say nowt. She's a rum woman, you know. Believes in sorting out her own battles. There's a lot to be said for keeping things to yourself.'

'Sometimes.'

'Ta-ra, Jack.'

'Ta-ra, Brad.'

Mosley went on his way. Just before the Mitregate crossing, a panda car drove up and the driver wound his window down.

'Got a minute, Inspector Mosley?'

It was Grimshaw, being driven by a constable new to the division, hence his scruples about the courtesies. He managed to get his long, ungraceful legs out of the car, and walked some way with Mosley.

'Strange times we live in,' he said.

Mosley always strictly rationed any appearance of co-operation with Grimshaw. He said nothing.

'I mean, there are crimes that hadn't been thought of when you and I were recruits. Like these damned silly kids.'

Mosley showed no curiosity about them.

'Glue-sniffing,' Grimshaw said.

He waited for Mosley to ask for an explanation. But Mosley did not reveal whether the term and the practice were new to him or not. There had, of course, been circulars about it. But no one in head office believed that Mosley ever read those.

'Some of the doctors reckon it's harmless. They'd do better to keep their mouths shut. It can lead to worse things. In any case, it's a damned nuisance. A lot of parents are worried out of their minds. Now we've a nasty one, out on the Cheviot Estate.'

'Who's that, then?'

'Lad called Watlington. Father's a finisher at Chadbolts'.'

'I know him. What's happened?'

'The silly young sods have found a new way of doing it. They soak the stuff into a bit of old rag, Scotch-tape it under their noses, then put a plastic bag over their heads. Young Watlington died of suffocation last night. Twelve years old.'

They had to wait for lights to let them over a crossing.

'No need for you to trouble yourself over it, though. Straightforward case for the coroner. I'll get Tyson over to give a talk at the school. He's Crime Prevention Officer, puts things over well with the kiddies. Of course, if you feel you ought to do that yourself, it's your territory –'

Mosley shook his head. Grimshaw wondered what, if anything, had registered. Glue-sniffing? Could Mosley possibly have heard of this bloody silly craze? They crossed the road, jumping outside the studs to avoid the bonnet of an orange Datsun whose driver hoped too much of the amber.

'I'll tell you what, though, Mosley. Find time to go round to the model shops and DIY places. Warn them to be on the look-out for non-genuine purchasers. Get the name of any kids they suspect.'

'I did that last week,' Mosley said.

Grimshaw stoped in mid-stride and grasped his elbow.

'There are times when I don't know what to make of you,' he said, 'I had to read this all up this morning.'

'You ought to watch more telly,' Mosley told him.

4

At the end of the afternoon Mosley went up to Hadley Dale on the school bus. An hour earlier he had been over to the school, but he did not go in. Last week he had called and given a list of names to the headmaster. Watlington's had been one of them. Some of the shopkeepers must have known that there were kids who could not possibly be making legitimate use of the glue in the quantity in which they were buying it. The headmaster had been polite, smooth – and unpersuaded. Now Mosley stood by the railings and looked into the yard with idle, middle-aged vacancy. It was a Middle School. The younger ones had not grown out of singing games.

The big ship sailed through the alley, alley-oh –

He remembered singing that one himself, when he had been that age. It gave him a sense of the continuity of time. The older boys were playing a game of forty-a-side asphalt football with an old tennis ball. Girls were skipping to a rhyme about Shirley Temple. Had they any idea who Shirley Temple was? One boy, under-developed for his years, was standing apart from everyone else, near a railed flight of steps that led down into a boiler-room. He looked miserable, isolated. At intervals he drew snivelling breath up a damp and suffering nose. For two or three minutes Mosley did not take his eyes off that boy.

He got a place on the school bus because the driver knew him. He sat behind the boy he had watched in the playground. The lad entered into no conversation with the child sitting next to him. He kept his face turned to the window, though he was probably seeing nothing. At intervals, he sniffed.

Elsewhere on the bus, the noise was so great that children were having to shout to their nearest neighbours. There was excited talk about the boy who had died. Excitement was the key-word, not grief. Only the child in front of Mosley seemed to have been driven out of his wits by what had happened.

'Mr Reynolds sent for three out of Mr Hall's class.'

'And Jackie Beavis and Dicky Bird out of Miss Jackson's.'

'Somebody must have told on Michael Turner. Mr Reynolds came and fetched him himself.'

Outside the Technical College, the bus stopped to pick up a handful of older students from outlying hill-country: jeans, sweat-shirts and chewing-gum. The bus stopped at crossroads and milk-platforms that were now mostly disused. Hadley village stood at the watershed of the Dale and there was a long, straight climb before the road twisted round a double hairpin under the first row of cottages. There were only three passengers left, and Mosley let them disappear into their homes before he himself moved in leisurely fashion along the broad main street. He made his way towards the end-cottage of a short terrace – a swept, flagged path, aluminium windows replacing former leaded lights. A woman was moving sloppily about her kitchen in ill-fitting mules.

Mosley knew that a lot of nonsense was talked about a policeman's sixth sense. What a policeman did need was experience: a stock of yardsticks, precedents, associations. May Hunter did not come immediately to the door when he knocked, and he knew that was because his visit did not come as an entire surprise to her, though she probably had a completely wrong idea of what it was about. He could hear her doing a frantic, flapping round of tidying up. The police, her mind would be telling her, were concerned with law and order, therefore they would be influenced by the state of law and order on kitchen shelves and living-room mantelpieces.

May Hunter was invariably harassed, even when there was nothing apparent to harass her. She had been pretty once, in a petite way that made her an improbable partner for Ted Hunter. But being married to him had dissolved her prettiness, superannuated it. Flesh and colour had shrunk away from her face. Her nose had become thinner and sharper, to the point at which it must have seemed a permanent accusation to the man who had to live with it. Not that Ted Hunter was a round-the-clock-and-calendar hellion. It was the drink – as he sanctimoniously repeated between bouts. He had both long and short spells of staying away from it.

'Mr Mosley?'

May Hunter could not hide her concern. It could not be good news when Mosley came visiting.

'It's your lad I wanted to talk to.'

'What's he done? He went up to his bedroom the moment he came into the house. He does nothing but moon about, these days. I don't know what to make of him. I can't do a thing with him. He hardly speaks to us. What's he been up to?'

Her eyes, rather than her nose, were the arresting features now – ridden with anxiety, yet capable of being vituperative.

'Better get him to tell us,' Mosley said.

She went to the stair-bottom and called the boy. Mosley looked round the room. There were one or two pictures on the walls, simplistic landscapes: the Lakes and a Cornish fishing village. The Hunters were not a bookish household: a greasy cookery manual, a *Family Doctor*, a *Road Atlas*, an unexpected *Book of Stately Homes*. Also unexpected was a row of half a dozen volumes in German: condensed novels, a schoolgirl's collection of Goethe's lyrics, a popular paperback edition of Dürer's woodcuts.

A full minute elapsed, and there was no answer from young Hunter.

'What's it all about, Mr Mosley?'

Then her temper gave out. She sprang halfway up the stairs and screamed for the boy. He came down as if he were afraid to take every next tread.

'What have you been doing with yourself, young Bernard? This is Inspector Mosley, the detective.'

Bernard remained near the foot of the stairs. Mosley called him over to the window, put two fingers under his chin and tilted his face up towards the light. He bent down to examine the skin under his nostrils.

'It's his hay fever,' his mother said.

'Sore, isn't it Bernard? Only it isn't hay fever, is it?'

The boy kept his defensive silence.

'It isn't, is it? It isn't hay fever?'

'I don't know.'

'What else could it be?'

The boy was too frightened to speak. Mosley turned to the woman.

'Glue,' he said quietly.

'Glue?'

'They sniff it,' Mosley said. 'It's a drug.'

'Oh, God, Bernard – you haven't, have you?'

Bernard grasped at a rationalization.

'I was leaning over a bench, and some of it went up my nose.'

Mosley took the boy's shoulders and pulled him round so that they were facing each other.

'I don't like boys who tell lies. And you're doing worse than telling lies to me. You're trying to tell them to yourself. A boy who would cheat himself would cheat anyone. You've been sniffing glue – like Jackie Beavis and Dicky Bird out of Miss Jackson's class – and Georgie Watlington. Tell your mother what happened to Georgie Watlington.'

No answer.

'Who's Georgie Watlington?' May Hunter asked.

'A lad from one of the Bradburn estates. He died yesterday. Glue-sniffing.'

'Oh, my God.'

She looked helplessly at both of them.

'His Dad will kill him. I daren't tell him. Does he have to know? Is there no way? Do you have to . . . ?'

Mosley looked at her as if he were extremely reluctant to stretch a point for her.

'What time does your husband leave for work in the mornings?'

'Half seven.'

'And what time does the post arrive?'

'Never before eight.'

'There'll be a letter from the school. Bound to be. It will be addressed to the boy's Dad. Get it before he sees it. Say nothing about it. If you have to go and see the headmaster, can you manage it without letting on?'

'I can make out I'm going for a hair-do.'

'I'd do that, if I were you, Mrs Hunter.'

She nodded, then turned and seized the boy by the sleeves of his jacket.

'What did you go and get mixed up in this sort of carry-on for?'

26

'Experiment and sensation,' Mosley said. 'And imitation.'

He moved forward now without making any excuses for himself and took one of the tattered text-books from the shelf. He chose the Goethe, whose archaic Gothic print meant nothing to him. He turned to the fly-leaf: *Charlotte Illing, Hildesheim, 1952*.

'Mr Longden's housekeeper was having a clear-out,' May Hunter said. 'She gave Ted a few books that she said might one day come in useful for Bernard.'

'When was this?'

'A few days ago. And I'll give the little bugger sensation. I'll give him imitation. I never know what's going on in his mind these days. I sometimes wonder if he's in his right mind. He's not like other lads. What's the betting he won't blurt this all out in front of his father even now?'

She pushed the boy away from her. Mosley took his leave.

There were strangers in the Plough and, from the equipment stacked in the corner, Mosley recognized them as the men Brad Oldroyd had told him about, who were surveying with theodolite and plane-table the depressions that the space vehicle was supposed to have made in the turf.

'Here's somebody you ought to meet, Mr Mosley.'

'Bloody interesting, this is. What was it you called them, sir? Railway lines?'

The group had fallen under the tutelage of Tom Appleyard (of sheep under mushroom fame) and Brad Oldroyd (forty-nine ghosts). Both were clearly in visionary mood.

'Mr Mosley'll be very interested, sir,' Tom Appleyard said, with a plum-palated respectability that no stranger would recognize as an affectation. 'Mr Mosley saw these things too. He went on telly about them.'

'I've been explaining to these people,' Brad Oldroyd said, shrewdly putting Mosley into the picture, 'how these television people happened to be here when this space-craft came down. We all saw that luminous thing in the sky, didn't we, Tom?'

'You saw it, too?' one of the strangers asked Mosley.

'I saw something.'

It had to be careful treading, when Appleyard and Oldroyd got going.

'It's fascinating. These points where the thing landed: we've plotted them carefully, and there's no doubt they're on an intersection of the prehistoric straight tracks. I don't know whether you're interested? I'm sure you've heard of ley lines?'

Mosley conveyed what they took to be a sense of agreement.

'Well, clearly this spot is the apex of a Pythagorean triangle whose hypotenuse runs through the old stone circle at Lower Brandreth, then directly under the altar of St John's Church at Hollow Row. And the base-line, which connects Broken Cross with Leaning Hill, if produced north-west, runs through the very spot where the northern extremity of this saucer, or whatever you like to call it, finally landed. Obviously they homed in on it.'

'Aye,' Tom Appleyard said, 'and if you stood in the dead middle of where they parked it, and drew a straight line through this pub, it would run like a plumb-line through the public bar of the Partridge at Ewedale, then six miles further on through the Hen and Chickens at Millstone Bridge. And it ends up – we know, because once when we were youngsters, Brad and I walked it with a compass – dead in front of Robert's Oyster Bar on Blackpool front.'

They were by nature a humourless bunch, and it took some seconds for it to dawn that their legs were being pulled. They were amateur scholars who took their specialism seriously – who had done enough reading of the received authorities to have mastered the jargon and mythology of their subject. But they had closed their minds to anything that might refute what they wanted to believe. One of them managed an unconvincing grin.

'Good joke, my friend, but . . .'

It was forced – and only barely tolerant.

'And did I understand that someone in the present company said that you were a policeman?'

'Aye, that's true.'

'With local responsibilities?'

'Detective-inspector,' Mosley said, keeping his voice low, as if he were saying something that was not known in the Plough.

He was aware of an exchange of looks between these men, of a whisper from one to the other.

'We think there's something you ought to see. Something else we found up on the hillside.'

At least they had the sense not to let Tom Appleyard and Brad Oldroyd hear this.

'If we could meet you outside – say in about five minutes' time – without drawing attention . . .'

They began to gather up their gear and vacate their seats, which was as well, because another gang of men was coming in: workers who had just knocked off in the quarry. Bernard Hunter's father was among them. It was pay night – a pint on the way home: four, five or six, more likely. The limestone dust in which they worked gave a convincing excuse of something to be slaked. Imitation and sensation: but hardly experiment. Ted Hunter was a coarsely big man, with an old-fashioned buckle-belt. If he did ever come to hear of the glue-sniffing, he would be the one to believe in bringing up a child in the way that he should go.

When Mosley came out of the pub, the ley-line enthusiasts had moved a little distance away.

'I'd hate to think we were leading you on a wild goose-chase, Inspector.'

'We thought at first, you see, that the thing might have tried to make a forced landing, and had scored up the ground. But come to think of it, it couldn't have got in amongst the trees without coming to damage. It's this way, Inspector – a bit of a rough climb for half a mile or so, I'm afraid.'

They conducted him along a lane that he knew well enough, leading past Matthew Longden's Hadley House, its façade expressionless and hard-hearted against the Pennine elements. Then they took a field-track that skirted a farmyard, crossed the corner of a rough meadow where store-cattle were pasturing and entered a small wood of beech, ash and oak. After five minutes of walking what was barely a footpath at all, the leader held a hand up for them to stop.

What he showed Mosley bore a close resemblance to a newly filled grave. The earth had been recently turned, and no effort seemed to have been made to conceal or camouflage it. Perhaps whoever had done it had been relying on the unlikelihood of visitors.

'We thought at first, you see, that their vehicle might have made some sort of ricochet before coming in for its final landing. But I can see now that that can't have been the case.'

'And then there was this.'

One of them had stooped down into the vegetation and picked up something that he had obviously handled before. It was a very damp, very dirty, very old-fashioned woman's hat, an irremediably misshapen creation in plaited straw.

'When did you discover this?' Mosley asked them.

'This afternoon – three to four hours ago.'

'Did you say anything about it in the pub?'

'No. We could see that would have been unwise. One of us went down to the village police-house, but the constable was out somewhere on duty. We were going to call on him again before we went home.'

They seemed to be in favour of fetching digging equipment straight away, and there was no lack of volunteers eager to do the work. They seemed generally disappointed in Mosley's lack of keenness: but Mosley knew that whoever was under that earth would still be there when Joe Ormerod came back from wherever he was. He managed to get the amateur archaeologists away from the site, and swore them to silence. He walked with them back down into the village and watched them drive off in their two cars before climbing the hill again to call on Matthew Longden.

5

Hadley Dale's sole imposing residence had become Matthew Longden's burning desire the moment it had come on the market. The house and the man had the same roots, the same robust contempt for showmanship. It was not very big, as country properties went. It had only five bedrooms, though they were large ones, and it stood in two acres of hillside, lightly wooded. There was no luxury here – and, especially, no show of luxury. Under earlier ownership there had been more extensive woodlands, and a farm on the flank of the supporting hill. But Longden had sold that off, neither wanting to manage it, nor believing that he could. There were some who said that it was the austerity of Hadley House that had finally driven Betty Longden to leave her husband, that he ought to have known that when he brought her there. But there was something about the property that Matthew could not resist. It did not make him lord of the manor. Hadley Dale did not acknowledge a squire. But who could tell what pretences were going on inside Matthew Longden's mind? Certainly he had been able to persuade himself that he was Hadley Dale's leading light; and he gave no one reason to dislike him.

The hour was still early as Mosley approached, but too late for it to be likely that Matthew Longden would be out of the house. Sometimes, even nowadays, he did try to potter pain-wracked in the immediate neighbourhood of the house, Lottie never far beyond call – but never when the chill of day's end was beginning to make itself felt.

Mosley approached directly, up the drive littered with fallen twigs. Ted Hunter did some of the heavier work about the estate out of quarry hours. But he achieved none of the fastidious neatness that Longden would have demanded in his more active years. The signs were that Longden knew these days that he had to be satisfied with what did get done.

As Mosley approached, Longden was standing in one of the

bay windows at the front of the house. He waved and moved towards the door of his sitting-room, opened it with his weight taken by the knob, came down the hall and let Mosley in. A moment later, he was gripping Mosley's hand in long fingers, hard, rather than sinewy; bones that it hurt him to move, knuckles that he could no longer straighten.

'It's been months, if not years, Inspector. Yet my spies tell me that you've been three times to Hadley Dale in the last six months without calling. You'll take a drop of something? Even if only to give me the excuse to take a drop myself?'

Baroque music was being played very loudly on an up-to-date stereo system. Longden turned the volume down – but not low enough to make intense conversation easy.

'I'm sure that whatever you've come for doesn't take precedence over Telemann.'

Whisky: like a poker bringing life to a fire that needs it at just that moment. Mosley took in the room. There was a cold tidiness about Matthew Longden's books, his records, his gleaming brass fender, his empty ashtrays, his uncrushed cushions. For years, between Betty and Lottie, he had looked after himself, and housekeeping had always been for him synonymous with regimentation. But he had never had any military experience; it was from book-keeping that he took his concepts of good order. One must suppose that in the last few years Lottie had introduced her own elements of warmth and living somewhere into the household. But Mosley looked round in vain for any residue of her influence in this room. There was not a picture, not an ornament that did not belong to Matthew Longden – not a vestige of reading, letter-writing or needle-work – not a suggestion that Lottie Pearson had ever shared this home. Had he kept her, then, to her own small corner of it?

Matthew Longden followed the movements of Mosley's eyes and interpreted them correctly.

'I know why you're here, Inspector. I know what you're looking for. You are under the impression that I am the sort of man who would allow my housekeeper to take over my living-room?'

So was he going to pretend that that was all she had been to him? Mosley knew him as a man of that kind of pride – a maker of the sort of moral image that could convince himself perhaps more than others. But his face did not entirely support his aplomb. Something was amiss with Matthew Longden. He was not looking exactly tortured, not quite disillusioned – and he almost always looked wearied these days. But Matthew Longden, who had always seemed to live above emotion, had been emotionally bludgeoned: Mosley thought – possibly.

There was not a soul in Hadley Dale who believed that Lottie Pearson had been no more to Matthew Longden than a housekeeper. One had only to see them together – and that not only in the early days – to know what they meant to each other. And besides, Lottie's reputation was not that of a woman who would stick for years to the kitchen and linen cupboard. No one doubted that she housekept to perfection. But it was not for that that she had come to the big house.

'She won't be coming back?' Mosley asked bluntly.

'I wouldn't take her back.'

There was no depth of feeling behind the statement. It was plain. It was true to the code that had always governed Matthew Longden. He was not a patient man, had never pretended to be. He was not a tolerant man, had never seen virtue in putting up with what he did not like.

The music played itself to a stop. The arm returned to its rest. Longden made no move to switch off the set. Every movement seemed to rack him – even reaching for his glass.

'When did she actually go?'

'Wednesday night. In the middle of the night – I can only suppose. She brought me my nightcap. I had to cook my own breakfast. And may I say that that is no novelty in my life?'

If there were any touch of bitterness about that, he might even have been satirizing himself.

'She had given you no hint that she was going?'

Matthew Longden spread helpless hands.

'Hint? I have never lived by dropping hints – nor wondering whether they are being dropped to me. If you mean, did she say she was leaving: no – she did not.'

'You did not hear her go?'

'Do you fancy that I lay awake at night listening in case she did?'

33

'I just wondered whether you heard any motor-car engine. You have no idea how she got away from the village?'

'I must assume that she had an accomplice. I am not unaware that there has been idle gossip about her and her attitude to men. It is common knowledge that she has had two disastrous marriages. I can believe that in some circumstances she would act on impulse rather than judgement. I have always told myself that this was none of my business. I remember talking to you when it was decided that she should live here. She was, and until Wednesday night remained, an ideal servant. You may remember that it had always been my intention to reward her generously.'

'How many of her belongings did she leave behind her?'

'None, except for a few trifles that I would imagine she intended to abandon. I have put those into an old case, which I will have taken down to her mother-in-law's if she does not claim it soon. Why are you asking questions in this tone, Inspector? Am I suspected of some criminality?'

'Not at all,' Mosley said. 'A woman has disappeared. I have always found it better to ask questions before memories are dimmed.'

'*Disappeared*, you say. That is making a melodrama of it. She has left. She left without giving the proper month's notice. What can I do about it – other than shrug my shoulders?'

'You have no idea where she can have gone? You had no reason at all to think that she possibly might?'

'Why should I?'

'Were you aware, at any time she was in your employ, that she had any contact of any kind with either of the two men in her life?'

'I naturally assumed not. But I did not read her letters nor have her followed when she went down to the village shop, or to see Mrs Pearson.'

Matthew Longden was letting it be seen – intended to let it be seen – that his patience was wearing thin. Mosley saw no point at this stage in allowing it to wear out.

He had known Longden for years. There had been a time when the two of them had had a good deal of respect for each other. They had first met when Longden was at the zenith of his profession, staid and influential, committee chairman of Rotary, honorary auditor of many of Bradburn's charity accounts, keeper of many men's financial secrets. His wife, of course, was still living with him in those days: a handsome, quiet woman, poised and generally liked. She was believed to have brought quite a share of money into their home from her distant roots in Shropshire. In the days when the couple had been living in Bradburn, it had been quite unthinkable that her eyes would ever falter towards another man.

Mosley was then a Detective-Sergeant, deeply entrenched in the subsoils of Bradburn. One day, Longden, chancing to meet him in the street, had asked him if he would drop in at his office when he could find the time. Mosley had found time immediately.

'Sergeant – more than one little bird has whispered to me that you're a man who knows how to be discreet.'

He obviously had something on hand that had to be managed discreetly. Longden paused, waiting for a reaction. Mosley waited, not giving any.

'What do you know about Ernest Weatherhead?'

Weatherhead was not quite the Uriah Heep of Bradburn. His desire to do a proper job was too genuine for that. And by anybody's standards, he was doing a proper job. In all but title he was manager of Raven's furniture shop in Cornmarket Street: not in title, because that might have implied that Roderick Raven ought to be paying him what he was worth.

'I've just finished Raven's accounts. A model in every respect but one. Roddy Raven doesn't know what a gem he's got in Ernest Weatherhead. You could use his ledgers to illustrate a text-book.'

Matthew Longden, not given to dramatization, was building up to something.

'There's only one thing spoils the picture. Ernie's short of cash in hand. Two hundred and fifty pounds, to make it a round sum. The last day's takings of the financial year.'

Mosley was silent for long enough to show that it had sunk in.

'What's Raven say about it?'

'I haven't told him. I've come to see you first.'

'Only Raven can initiate action, of course.'

'Which he won't. The scandal would be bad for trade. There'd be no point in being awarded costs that Weatherhead couldn't pay. But he'd sack Weatherhead. And the word would go round: the Chamber of Commerce, the Masons. Weatherhead would be lucky to get a job wheeling a barrow.'

Longden was studying every nuance in Mosley's eyes, looking for trust – or contra-indications. They were not sure of each other yet.

'To Roderick Raven, two hundred and fifty is nothing. For Ernest Weatherhead, it's unattainable. I like the young man,' Longden said. 'I could help him out – but I don't know whether I ought to. I want to know what he's been up to, and why. And I don't want it to get round that I'm going soft. I am not suggesting for a moment, Sergeant, that you do something of which your superiors would disapprove. But you have a certain reputation – a wind that bloweth not where it listeth not . . .'

Mosley considered it. He would have a look, anyway. But he was not sure how much he would tell Longden of what he found.

'I'm not asking you to commit yourself in advance, Sergeant. If what you discover seals your lips – or demands inevitable action, you must do as you see fit. But if Weatherhead's troubles are genuine – if he could be saved by an interest-free loan – and if his attitude is reasonable – I might be tempted to make an unorthodox move. It wouldn't do, of course, for any of my other clients to get wind of it.'

'It'll take me a day or two,' Mosley said.

'Thank you, Sergeant. I take it that elementary book-keeping is no problem for you?'

'It's largely a matter of common sense, I would think.'

'It can need uncommon sense, if someone's trying hard enough to lose an item. Ernest Weatherhead's columns are plain enough for a child to follow. Could you spend an hour or two with this little lot, see if your conclusions agree with mine? I may say it's touch and go, when I know someone as well as I know Ernest, whether I actually ask to see the inside of the safe. I don't know what prompted me to this time.'

Mosley did not find the task difficult. He had a long interview with Ernest Weatherhead that did not go into his official notebook. One day towards the end of the previous June, Weatherhead had made a fundamental change in his working routines. Up to now he had always paid the takings into the bank through a night-safe at the end of each working day. Then he had started taking in his paying-in book during the course of the morning – with the previous day's receipts. From now on, his banking was consistently a day behind. And Ernest Weatherhead was a day's takings – approximately £250 – in pocket. He had been unable to make up the deficit by the end of the financial year.

Mosley knew the young man, knew his wife, his and her family. Ernest Weatherhead was what they called locally a *worriter*: trivial details could obscure his larger view. It was easy to picture the torment he must have been through. The sum was small enough for him to have had some hope, in the first months, of making it good: by a windfall or a bet. Weatherhead was not normally a betting man, but he made one catastrophic experiment. He even had some hope at first from cheese-paring weekly savings – but domestic emergencies swallowed up the lot. And the whole thing was because of his wife's first baby. She had insisted, to the brink of hysteria, on a private nursing home: an extravagance over which the town of Bradburn had clucked. Margaret Weatherhead had heard scarey stories about the NHS maternity wards. Young married women got on each other's nerves with their bitchy tales.

It was no trouble to Mosley to get at the details. The young man's hands were trembling when he was asked to call at the accountant's offices to collect his books. There were tears – it embarrassed Longden to look at the man. But he was psychologist enough to let the suffering go on for some time before he let it be known that he was prepared to act as fairy godfather.

That had not been the end of the matter. Weatherhead had paid back Matthew Longden to the penny and to the day. But Longden had never let him forget the episode. If ever he came into Raven's shop, Weatherhead wanted to hide. Longden had a way of looking at him that was a perpetual reminder. When the books came in for annual audit, it was not beyond him to remark that he hoped that Mr Mosley wouldn't have to show an interest this year.

'Honestly, Mr Mosley,' Weatherhead once said to him, 'I sometimes wish I'd been found out and faced the music. At least it would have been over and done with.'

But for Matthew Longden, nothing was ever over and done with. He had been magnanimous. He knew he had been magnanimous. He prided himself on what he had done for Ernest Weatherhead. It was another act of magnanimity to add to his personal capital.

Mosley looked at him now, exercising his exemplary patience – which threatened to reach exhaustion point at any moment. But the outburst did not come. Instead, Matthew Longden took solace in a bout of self-pitying irony.

It had seemed to the world – to two worlds, Bradburn and Hadley Dale – an exemplary marriage. Then his wife had gone off with some man whom she had apparently been seeing for some time. It had been a shock that neither Bradburn nor Hadley Dale had found it easy to assimilate. Betty Longden was a tall, serene, altogether rather splendid woman from a part of the country of which Hadley Dale knew nothing but imagined a good deal that was unsubstantiated. She had been a paragon of courtesy to everyone she met, yet there had been some barrier that had prevented anyone from getting to know her – as Hadley Dale understood getting to know people. It was not quite the same sort of thing as prevented people from getting to know her husband. In his case, it was his convincing sense of superiority. In hers, it was something totally elusive. Mosley had wondered, while the period of speculation had been at its most feverish, how well even her husband had known her.

'Of course, I'm no stranger to being left to my own resources,' Longden said to Mosley now, not without quiet enjoyment of his own martyrdom.

At least he was not asking Mosley to start looking for Lottie Pearson. When his Betty had wandered off, he had stirred up the pot and kept the sediment in suspension for months. He had employed and dismissed three private detectives in succession to try to get after her traces. He had almost ruptured blood-vessels in his fury against the police, whose certainty clearly was that she was an adult female who had gone her own way and was breaking no laws. They did not believe her to be in any danger, and they were obviously not bestirring themselves to look for her. Then had come one of those fortuitous strokes that sometimes cut corners. Betty Longden, making a phone call from a kiosk in the Greater Manchester area, had left behind her in the booth a booklet of airline tickets. It looked as if she had been calling the airline to confirm a check-in time. The tickets, which bore her name, were found by the next man to use the box, and he handed them in at a police station. No one there connected her with a missing person, and the duty officer informed the airline company at the airport. It was the next day before a police clerk spotted that she was a listed person – and by then there was no more to do than to confirm against the passenger manifest that she had already departed for Amsterdam on a single ticket. Longden had despatched the latest of his private eyes to Holland, but there had been no trail there to be picked up.

Longden, still lingering over the image of how meanly the fates had treated him, offered Mosley more Scotch. Mosley declined.

'Do you remember how I talked to you about it, when Mrs Pearson first moved in here?'

Mosley had known at the time that he was being used as nothing more than a baffle-board for Longden's own thoughts. There was nothing unorthodox about a man's taking a housekeeper. It was as safe a way as existed for a man like Longden to take a mistress. Yet somehow, Longden had needed to talk about it, and it had not been lost on Mosley that the retired accountant was more deeply affected by the woman than he would admit. The only personal thing he had said about her was to praise her for her musicality. That, Longden had thought, stemmed from her nationality. How many people in Hadley Dale would have been as moved by J.S. Bach as Lottie Pearson was?

Mosley had limited himself to saying that he was sure Longden was doing a sensible thing. He ought to have had help in the house years ago. And if he had been able to find a woman to share his interests – Longden lived for his stereo – so much the better. Of course, clacking tongues here and there would jump to peevish conclusions – but what did that matter? A month from now, Mosley told him, the idea of Mrs Pearson living at Hadley House would be as natural a part of the status quo as if she had always lived there.

At the same time, Mosley had noted that Lottie Pearson was a sensuous and potentially sensual woman. He had no reason to think of her as morally loose, but he thought she might be morally flexible. She would never have sold herself, but he fancied she might be the type of woman who would give herself generously and without much judgement. She was obviously a woman who had enjoyed men in her time, and had an appalling track-record of being blind to their faults until she was entangled with them. That was what had happened in the case of her first husband, an English private soldier in the Rhine army, whom she had probably regarded as a triumphant capture at the time. There had undoubtedly been something romantic in their linguistic difficulties, and through him she would have gained entry into a set that would have made her the envy of some German girls. There would have been madcap beery nights out. It was not until he had brought her to England that she realized what she had come down to. When he started knocking her about, she forgave him a time or two: the task of standing on her own feet in a foreign country still looked a formidable one, and she was too proud to want to go home disillusioned. But eventually he abandoned her – in Bradcaster. That was where she met Jack Pearson – with whom she was to fare no better. Anyone in Hadley Dale, not excepting Jack's mother, would have forecast that for her without hesitation.

Then after Jack Pearson, after living on for another eighteen months with his mother, came Matthew Longden. It was not difficult to see what illusions she might have had about him.

'So she got herself involved with that crew from the TV company?' Mosley asked casually, and as if his sympathies all lay with Longden.

Longden snorted. 'I make no bones about it. I was furious with her. It was all so cheap. She threw herself at that producer as if she had not set eyes on a man in ten years.'

There was a limit to what Mosley could afford to reveal. He must not know about the sand in her porridge. That would be letting down Percy Allnut, *Chymist*.

The interference with the wheel-nuts on the car, on the other hand, was something that it was safe for him to know about, since Ted Hunter had been involved. Hunter was certain to have been indiscreet in the Plough. There was no point in protecting the confidences of Plough talk.

'She sometimes drove your car, didn't she? Hadn't you taught her yourself?'

'That was in the early days, before I came to know her properly. It's a decision I've often regretted.'

'Wasn't there something to do with the wheels?' Mosley said suddenly. 'Something about nuts being loose, and a hub-cap off?'

And there was no doubt that this caught Longden like a blow to the side of the head. The blood flushed up under the scaly skin of his cheeks and he momentarily caught his breath.

'How do you know about that?'

'Talk.'

Longden paused a second. 'I should have known. Not my cleverest moment. Not a thing I'd do if I'd my time over again.'

'It was your doing?'

'I told Hunter to do it. I had no intention of harming her. That's why I insisted on his leaving the cap off the wheel, lying where she would see it – so there was no danger she'd try to drive off. I felt certain she wouldn't know how to use a wheel-brace – or even that there is such a thing. It was just bad luck that Hunter was still about the place. Of course, he had no alternative but to tighten the nuts for her.'

'And what was it all about?'

Longden took a slow, deep breath. There was a strong suggestion in his eyes that any moment now he was going to start objecting to these questions. But – almost visibly – he applied himself to this one.

'I might as well tell you. I didn't paint the whole picture just now. She'd been speaking for some months of leaving. And I'd told her that as far as I was concerned, I'd rather she made up her mind about it than go on talking about it. What I didn't want was her going off with the car. I'm not suggesting for a moment, Inspector, that she would have stolen it: not to

41

deprive me of it for good. She'd have left it where I could have picked it up, once it had taken her where she wanted to be. In the meantime, I would have been putting up with God knows what inconvenience.'

'And why was she threatening to go?' Mosley asked.

Again came the pause that was a danger sign. And again Longden disciplined himself. 'Because she' was getting above herself. Because being the best paid and most indulged servant in the western hemisphere was insufficient for her. Because she to whom thou givest shall ask for more. Because the novelty had worn off. Because it bored her to have to run a household in my way. Because it would have suited her better to turn Hadley House into a cross between a mausoleum and a Teutonic social history museum. Because if I asked for a four-minute egg, and she thought a three-minute egg was better for me, a three-minute egg was what I got.'

Outside, the light was beginning to fade. Beyond the tops of the trees the sky was dissolving into a uniform dark blue. Joe Ormerod would have come home for his supper by now. The beetle-browed constable did not yet know what sort of a night he was in for. Mosley had to go and tell him that he had a date on a hillside, once it could be assumed that Hadley Dale had gone to bed: a date with a spade.

'No. It hadn't been working for some months – which was a pity. Because at her best, Mrs Pearson was a hard worker, and until she began to need variety, as contented to be here as I was to see her about the place. However . . .'

Longden was going dismally on, self-righteous, and obviously under no doubt that he was justifying himself. Mosley terminated the conversation and stood up. They promised each other that they would keep each other posted with anything there was to report. Despite the excruciating business of getting his limbs into motion after so long at rest, Longden insisted on seeing Mosley to the door. And when Mosley had gone no more than twenty yards along the drive, he heard music so loud that it seemed to be breaking through the stone-work of the house.

Over to Joe Ormerod then, to alert him. And then Mosley had another call to make before the melodramatic side of the night's activities started.

6

So what did Mosley really know about Lottie Pearson? What people said, interpreted in the light of what they might be expected to say. People said about her what they did say about Germans, forgetting two world wars: that she worked like a Trojan and ate like a famished horse. That she had a wandering eye for a man, but that no man in Hadley Dale had let his eyes wander in her direction – except Jack Pearson and Matthew Longden, as unlikely a pair to speak of in the same breath as any man could imagine. That she had married a good-for-nothing who had blackened her eyes and abandoned her in Bradcaster. That it was in Bradcaster that she had met Jack Pearson who, anyone could have told her, would go on to treat her even worse than the last one did. That she seemed constitutionally incapable of resisting the temptation to 'help' any man who appeared to need help. Then Jack Pearson had also departed from her life, and it was confidently reported that it was old Sarah and Lottie working in concert who had given him his marching orders, since when it had been love and hate all the way between Lottie and Sarah. There were goose-pimpling stories of the screaming rows that went on between them, but this could not have been the whole story, because both women were free agents. Sarah had shown no signs of kicking Lottie out, and Lottie had given no inkling that she wanted to up sticks: until she and Matthew Longden caught sight of each other, and Matthew Longden saw which side his bread was buttered.

Mosley went briefly to see Joe Ormerod, and then, until such time as the communal curiosity of Hadley Dale had reached the snoring stage, dropped over to chat with old Sarah. Because old Sarah was going to be the key to many things – if only he could coax them out of her before she took it into her head to kick him out into the night.

It was between nine o'clock and half past and old Sarah was

getting ready to go to bed, an old country widow's habit that did her no good at all, since she was making her first pot of tea by five every morning and had her vigorous round of household *fettling* completed by seven, leaving herself a fruitless morning of pottering about. Sarah Pearson was a woman who for various complex reasons liked all people to think she looked on them as enemies. For some equally extraordinary reason, she always seemed ready to admit Mosley to her councils. Perhaps this was because she thought that the nature of his work qualified him to share her contempt for humanity.

She made no difficulty about admitting him now, though at the moment when he knocked she was at her front door involved in her final day's fury with bolts and chains. She had raked out her fire and damped down what embers remained: she had a vivid anticipation of every possible type of catastrophe. Her living-room, like herself, was a compound of personalities. There was a mantel photograph of Edwardian parents in all the self-conscious solemnity of the lowest respectable stratum of the rural working class. There was a framed postcard of her son Jack in the uniform of a 1939 militiaman – taken, actually, between two spells in the glasshouse. There was a tradesman's calendar several years old that she had preserved presumably because its picture appealed to her: an Olde Englishe rustic ford, bridge and willow. Her furnishings were threadbare but clean: dust was given little chance to settle in her house.

'You must be ruddy barmy, you must,' she said, establishing in advance that however friendly and helpful she might feel, she was not going to show it.

'What have I done now?' Mosley asked, with the right shade of comic resignation.

'Carrying all that lumber for me down to the bus. I hear enough about myself now, without being seen to be friends with a copper. So you've come at last, have you? About time, too. If you ask me, he's done away with her – same as he did with his first wife.'

Her tone admitted of no doubt on these issues. But it would need an hour or two of subtle patience to find out whether she had any useful evidence to offer. Mosley nodded as if he had known all along, of course, that both accusations were true. They sat chatting like a pair of old friends in a vintage parish magazine illustration.

'You could hardly call Lottie his wife,' he said tentatively.

'You don't reckon they sat listening to his gramophone all night, do you?'

'How did she fall in with him in the first place?'

'It was when everybody had the flu, wasn't it? It was that young fly-by-night from the Bradburn Welfare, wasn't it, who came bellyaching for someone to go up and do for him.'

'Was it?'

Sitting in her rocker with her hands folded in her lap, Sarah Pearson's head nodded like a foraging hen's as she told her story.

Her daughter-in-law had started working as a home-help up and down the village and her name had quickly been put on the roster of official workers. To hear Sarah Pearson talk, one would think that she had never had anything but unqualified admiration for the woman. And it was not difficult imagining the *blitzkrieg* that had been waged in some squalid old men's cottages.

'A tip, Jonathan Clegg's was, Mr Mosley. The sort of house where you wiped your feet when you came out. Until Lottie read him the riot act. He'd a saucepan of fat on his cooker that looked like a moss-garden. She had the place so you could eat off the floor.'

Then had come the epidemic. It had taken to their graves more than one of the old people that Lottie had looked after. Worse than that, it had laid low many of her fellow-workers in the field. The medical officer had come pleading with Lottie to go and 'sort out' Matthew Longden, who could not be taken into the cottage hospital because so many of the nursing staff had been struck down that all admissions had been suspended.

It was a March day, rain slashing in leaden spears across the dismal deserted theatre of the village square. The smoke hung low and amorphously over the cottage roofs, as if it were more than it could do to struggle up through the elements.

'You'd be mad to go,' Sarah Pearson told her, but Lottie was already putting on her German-looking hat, buttoning her outdoor coat across her well-found bosom. The welfare woman ran her up to the big house in her car. But it was late in the evening before she returned, and that was on foot, through rain driven by a near-gale. She had scarcely been able to stand up in it, had been able to make progress, she said, only by walking backwards with a stoop. And even at that, until she had mastered the art of leaning into the wind, her shoulders had been jostled against wall-ends and gateposts. Lottie Pearson was a tough woman, but she had had to sit by the fire for several minutes before she even wanted to start taking her coat off.

Sarah Pearson berated her for her foolishness. There was no man on earth who was worth that degree of exhaustion, least of all Matthew Longden, who had enough egg on his chin for a chamberful of district councillors. But Lottie insisted that she must go back there tomorrow. Old Sarah put on a very creditable imitation of her mish-mash of accent and idiom.

'Ze poor old bugger have need of ze hands of ze woman.'

'You watch out he doesn't have need of something more than your hands,' Sarah told her.

'Ach, zat! He is too weak to piss,' said Lottie, whose instruction in the English tongue had been broadly based.

And the next morning, without lingering even to make a proper breakfast, she had insisted on going back up to Hadley House, though there seemed to have been no abatement of the storm. Moreover, she had filled her basket from their joint larder with an abandon that Sarah described to Mosley with lurid resentment.

'*Ach, was!* He have money. I go to ze shop on ze way home.'

Lottie Pearson was away for the inside of a long day, came back in darkness, and was shivering to the core of her body as she sat with her knees burning in front of Sarah's well-stoked fire. Lottie was one of those women who always escape epidemics in their early and middle stages, when the majority of the populace have succumbed. It is only when the rest of the world is recovering that they are stricken – and badly. Sarah Pearson had no doubt of the symptoms, but Lottie would still not admit them to herself.

'I can see myself nursing you through double pneumonia,' Sarah told her.

The old woman must have been speechless with exasperation to see Lottie facing the weather on yet a third day, with nothing inside her but a cup of tea, which she barely gave herself time to finish. She did not come home again at all that day – and sent no message, because there was no way in which a message could have been carried. But Sarah made no allowances for that. She had sat up till nearly eleven, waiting to lock up. From the way she told the story, it did not seem that she had forgiven Lottie for that yet. But the milkman, Bill Henry, brought a note the next morning. It was in Matthew Longden's handwriting, not at its most firm, and it announced that it would be a day or two before Lottie would be fit to come home.

It was not quite a case of the blind leading the blind. Necessity sometimes draws strengths out of unexpected reserves. Lottie Pearson had nursed Matthew to the stage at which he could just about get up and go to the lavatory. Seeing the state that his nurse was in, he had struggled downstairs, and now it was his turn to concoct the sweat-making drinks. Lottie Pearson was not now in a state to deny that she needed them.

It was all of ten days before Matthew Longden drove her back down into the village. It was not a question of verbal warfare with Sarah Pearson now; the pair were speechless with hostility.

'So when are you moving in with him for good?' old Sarah asked.

It was not until the day after her return that Lottie announced that henceforth she was going in daily to look after Mr Longden: in point of fact, he had told her that she must let at least two weeks go by before she thought of working again. Embittered and critical, her mother-in-law observed how she dressed up for what was supposed to be a charring session in her best lacquered straw bonnet, which she adjusted several times in front of the mirror. God knows where she had acquired it. It might have been fashionable in the more conservative German provinces before the last war.

'What time am I to expect you back this time, then? Have I to keep you a supper?'

'I don't know. I don't know whether Mr Longden will ask me to share a bite with him.'

Which he did – and to stay for tea, as well as sit at his midday table. There was a complexity of sarcasm from Sarah Pearson's lips. She had no room at all for Matthew Longden at the best of times. Mosley found it difficult to be clear about the reasons for this. It was partly class hatred, inbred – and with a lifetime of continuous reinforcement. But Sarah Pearson was also repetitive about the way he had treated his wife. What form this had taken, and how she came to be so sure of it were things to which Mosley found it difficult to track his way to a satisfactory answer.

'You could see the poor woman had no soul to call her own.'

But how could she see such a thing?

'It was written all over her face, even if you only saw her for a minute in Madge Rowley's shop.'

What, exactly, was written in her face?

'She wasn't part of the place – and you could see that she wanted to be. She was always itching to hurry back to the big house. You could see that she wanted to stand and talk, but it was as if she was scared to be late back.'

Mosley knew Sarah Pearson and her sort too well to think that their case was weakened, just because they could not be articulate about it. One thing was clear: Lottie had not worried about how late she came back home. She was soon spending more time with Matthew Longden than she was with Sarah.

'Started staying to supper, too, if you please. Listening to music. *Real* music she tried to tell me.'

Sarah nodded towards her all-mains pre-war cabinet radio.

'We always listened to "Friday Night is Music Night". I never knew her go on about that.'

But Matthew Longden had several hundred pounds' worth of high technology.

'Beethoven and that. She cracked on there was something special about her when it came to music.'

One night she came home outrageously late from something they had been listening to together.

'Red spots over her cheeks. That excited. I could tell.'

Clearly this was the definitive crisis between the two. Two days later, Lottie made it known that Matthew Longden had asked her to be his resident housekeeper and that she would be taking all her lumber up the hill as soon as she could get Harry Wheeldon to shift it for her in his van.

'And the next the village knew, he was teaching her to drive his car. His housekeeper! Dressed to the nines at the steering-wheel as if she were on her way to open some garden fête. You'd think she was gentry, to see her driving round the countryside. It hadn't been often that we'd seen Matthew Longden outside his own grounds, especially since his wife died. But now it was all day up in the dales, a day in the Trough, a trip out to Scarborough.'

And life had settled down to a rhythm with which many people were familiar, not forgetting their shopping expeditions on Friday mornings. Whatever venom Sarah Pearson might strew over the evidence, however piously Matthew Longden might pretend it had only been a master–servant relationship, Mosley knew that there had been a time when the two had taken such pleasure in each other's company that they had not cared who had seen it. Matthew Longden had made a settlement on Lottie Pearson such as men only make on their wives. Those who were sympathetic to both parties had believed that here were two people who had had the good fortune to be compensated for their leaner years. And there had appeared nothing grotesque in their relationship. Lottie Pearson was a comely woman. Matthew Longden never cut less than a gentlemanly figure. And at the height of their friendship, their very happiness made them a pleasant pair to see together.

So when had the first signs been noticed that things were cooling between them? It was not a point on which Sarah Pearson could be helpful. She had been too delighted that things had cooled.

'What about your Jack? Did he never make any effort to get in touch with her?'

She looked at Mosley as if she doubted his sanity.

'He'd know better than to try to come here.'

'Has he been seen at all about the village?'

'Do you think he dare? There'd be too many wanting to settle with him.'

Jack Pearson was capable of sparkling good humour. Some of his catch-phrases might even sound witty, to someone as strange to the vernacular as Lottie Pearson. He had always had a strong taste for contemporary fashion: much of the dishonesty that got him in trouble from time to time was to finance his sartorial conceits. The photograph of him in wartime uniform, which his mother – oddly enough – had not thrown away, showed a cheap, common, yet fastidious Adonis. But when it came to petty crime, his absolute lack of intelligence showed through. He was incapable of imagining himself ever caught. He could not think that his current scheme was not foolproof. And in last ditches – in which he found himself regularly – he was capable of incredible and futile meanness. He did not understand the nature of debts of friendship. If somebody else could be caused to carry a can for him, he gave no thought for loyalties of the past, or investments that he might need for the future.

The last time he left home and Lottie Pearson, he had disappeared in the direction of Bradcaster, presumably into the twilit world of sleazy lodgings. It must certainly have come somehow to his knowledge that Lottie had gone to live at the big house. Could he have avoided the temptation to find his way to her there, a begging visit, pitching an all too credible hard-luck story? And could Lottie Pearson, with her weakness for underdogs, have resisted giving him at least some help, however shabbily he had dealt with her before?

There was no answer to that here. Old Sarah would not know. Mosley looked at the time. Sarah Pearson kept her clock permanently ten minutes fast, as if there was something that she was perpetually in danger of missing, as if her profound distrust in her environment extended even to escapements and pendula.

'You're off, then?' she said, noticing his stirrings. 'I've squared it all up for you, have I?'

'Squared?' Mosley asked. 'Squared? Who's got any right-angles in Hadley Dale?'

7

There were certain things you had to bear in mind when you were exhuming a corpse. One was that you did not know how deep the thing was likely to lie. Very often whoever had disposed of it had been glad of the time he could save himself by skimping the depth. You did not want to go driving in the point of your pick just where you would add to the pathologist's uncertainties. And this was especially true when the cadaver had been in the earth as short a time as might be the case with Lottie Pearson: only since Tuesday, and today was only Friday. You didn't want to go stabbing the edge of your spade into flesh that was at that early stage of decomposition.

The other thing you need is a rigid control of your imagination. You have to keep your mind on what you are doing, but not let it dwell on certain aspects: even detective-inspectors have their human susceptibilities. It had not come Mosley's way to take part in many disinterments, and it was a long time since the last one. But he had in his time exposed both old bones and fresher flesh. In every case they had belonged to someone he had not known. When you are familiar with what used to be someone, you learn to look at things obliquely. Joe Ormerod, on the other hand, had never performed this kind of duty before. He went at it with a brute energy that Mosley had to curb.

'Just remember, Joe, she may only be a foot or so under. We don't want to damage her more than she's been damaged. At the very first sign that we've made contact, we don't go on digging, we don't even scrape – we start brushing soil away as if we were dusting the best china. She won't have the protection of a casket.'

Joe had accepted the chore characteristically – with neither complaint nor any show of interest. Mosley had had to keep him quiet as they trudged through the Hadley Dale night. It was a struggle to keep digging gear from clanking. It would be a mighty feat to do what they were setting out to do without the knowledge of Hadley Dale, but they had to achieve that if possible. Mosley even refused to allow them to use lights until they were on the blind side of a wall that bounded Matthew Longden's estate. Their progress was uneven, and accompanied by mutterings from Joe that did not seem to be an actual form of communication. Eventually they reached the spot to which the ley-line seekers had taken Mosley. He lit and deployed all their lamps and lanterns – they had to take a chance now – and began testing top-soil gingerly with a pick. He was conscious enough of his age to know that Joe would have to do most of the heavy work, and, once Joe started digging, it was not a question of urging him on, but of slowing him down, cajoling him to have a proper respect for what he was doing.

Suddenly Joe straightened himself up, put his hand on his stomach, then bent forward again, away from the shallow trench he had already made. He began retching.

'What is it, Joe?'

'I'm into something. I think it might be her neck.'

He heaved again.

'Let me,' Mosley said, and fell on his knees beside the spot where Ormerod had been working. He felt with his fingers, plunged them into something wet and cold.

'Pass me one of the trowels, Joe. You can leave this to me.'

He began to edge the soil gently aside, felt his spade catch presently against fabric.

'Here she is, Joe. Not more than eighteen inches down. Thank God for small mercies. He wasn't very respectful, was he? Damn it, it's a wonder the foxes haven't found her.'

Grave-digger's humour, path. lab. cynicism, undertaker's callousness: you had to let yourself go to take your mind off the true meaning of what you were unearthing. You mustn't let your mind dwell on the last time you saw Lottie Pearson: at Bradburn market, smiling her special sideways smile at Matthew Longden – and Longden smiling back at her.

'At least, he had the decency to wrap her in a blanket. That was probably so he didn't have to keep catching sight of her himself. And blast it, Joe, the overlap is tucked in underneath her. We shall have to expose the whole surface before we can get at her.'

Joe Ormerod had quickly recovered.

'Shall I get working at the other end, then, Mr Mosley?'

'Aye, lad. Let's make half the work of it.'

Joe got down on his knees at the other end of the mound and started working as Mosley was, not actually digging, but gently easing away soil. A waning moon was just beginning to clear a skyline stretch of trees, and soon they could see remarkably clearly all they were doing. Every time one of their hands touched a blanket, they were within a fraction of an inch of what had been Lottie Pearson.

'You know what, Mr Mosley? I don't think there is a body under this thing.'

'You may be right, Joe. I'm beginning to wonder myself. Let's hope that it isn't – unless that means that she's buried somewhere else – deeper.'

It was the right size and shape for a body – the right size and shape for Lottie Pearson's body. But once they had the upper contour of the blanket exposed, it was obvious that something was wrong somewhere. In places the content was too soft, in others too hard and angular.

'No, Joe. This is not Lottie Pearson. We'd better see what it is we have got.'

They now had to scrape soil from under the blanket, which slowed them down. What they finally brought up into the moonlight was a pile of clothing – a woman's clothing – underwear, blouses, summer frocks, skirts, jumpers. There were other things, too: a couple of cheap, touristy pictures of castled crags in the Rhine Valley, a few long-playing records, singles, German pop hits of the 1960s. If someone had wanted to clear out of his sight everything belonging to a woman whom he now hated, the result would be just such a collection.

Ormerod began assembling their implements.

'Hey, wait a minute, Joe. We haven't finished yet. There could be a bit of a trick here. She might be under this lot. This might only be the top of the dressing.'

But it was not. The soil became firmer. Their spades caught into a root system that had not previously been disturbed.

There had been no digging deeper than the bed on which the blanket had lain. Mosley insisted that they shift the soil back into the trench. It needed a double journey to carry their tools and their booty back down to the police-house.

'So what have we learned, Joe?'

Ormerod looked at him with eyes that seemed more than usually witless.

'Quite right, Joe. We've learned nothing. We don't know whether she's alive or dead.'

He got the constable to run him home. The cats' eyes of the highroad undulated, swung smoothly round curves, were swept away behind them. The roads were free of traffic. Ormerod drove with his foot firmly down, but with steady control. He ignored village speed limits. Mosley did not complain.

He was in fact beginning to be overwhelmed by waves of fatigue. He was not so much constantly falling asleep as constantly being jerked awake. At one point he wiped steam away from the window – Ormerod had actually changed down to negotiate the zigzagging narrow street of Crawdon: not Mosley's responsibility, an enclave of Chief Inspector Marsters's territory. He saw three men step back into shadows at their approach: Bertie Lee from Strubshaw Bottoms, Alf Carter from Gunley. Both had spent a substantial proportion of their inadequate lives under lock and key. It was bad to see them in each other's company, even more suggestive that they should be as far from their natural haunts as Crawdon. But the worst feature of all was that the third man in the company should be Jack Pearson.

But Mosley's eyes fell shut again. Ormerod challenged his shock-absorbers as he hurled them at the hump-back bridge at Crawdon End. For once in a while, Mosley let duty recede into the night.

8

A report had to be written, and Mosley's was succinct, clear, factual and suppressed anything in the nature of theorizing. He made no attempt to suggest any conclusions, restricting himself austerely to material facts as actually known.

Detective-Superintendent Tom Grimshaw decided to suspect foul play and mounted a forward tactical headquarters at Hadley Dale, telling the ACC that even if this proved ultimately to have been an extravagance, it was no bad thing to set the machine up and let freshly lubricated cogs turn once in a while.

Men with whippy sticks flogged the grass and undergrowth of the woodlands and hillsides. Savage-fanged dogs were allowed to sniff at the clothes that had belonged to Lottie Pearson, and scampered off inanely to follow trails over Matthew Longden's estate and its surrounds: without result.

The same garments were subjected to every ingenuity of contemporary technology in forensic laboratories. A great deal of information was deduced as to their age, provenance and the length of time that they had been in the ground. Much was learned of the history of Lottie Pearson's lingerie, but nothing whatever about its owner's present whereabouts.

Tom Grimshaw himself interviewed Matthew Longden at great length, and when he had finished, the Superintendent exchanged views with Mosley about the man. It was obvious that Grimshaw had been very favourably impressed indeed by Longden, a man after his own heart, of whose sort there were not nearly enough left in the world today. Mosley received this opinion with a lack of emotion that might possibly have denoted concurrence, but did not volunteer to expand his own thoughts on the subject in any way.

It was Mosley's right, according to the manuals, since all this was taking place in his operational area, to be kept informed of all phases of the exercise, and to be available for consultation on all issues that might require a local guide. His own part in the actual investigation was restricted to leading a team that filled in a questionnaire to be answered by every man, woman and child in Hadley Dale who could be contacted. There were three main questions. Had they seen anything at all of Lottie Pearson after the departure of the television company? Had they heard anything out of the ordinary on any night last week? And when was the last time that they had seen Lottie Pearson, spoken to her, or seen anyone else speaking to her? The results were so negative that it seemed as if no one in Hadley Dale had even known the woman.

Then, Lottie Pearson's name by now having climbed into the news, a message was transmitted from a police station in the Greater Manchester area.

On Thursday of last week, a man had called in at that station bringing a folder of airline tickets that had been inadvertently left in a telephone kiosk. It rather looked as if Lottie had been ringing the airport to confirm a check-in time. The duty officer had contacted the airline desk, and it seemed as if Lottie Pearson had also done the same thing as Betty Longden, for the passenger manifest showed her as having flown to Amsterdam at about the same hour on the Friday as Mosley had been watching for her in Bradburn.

The forward tactical headquarters was dismantled, the co-operation of the Dutch police was promised and Mosley again became the undisputed king-pin in his area. One weekday morning not long after this, that area became involved in a man-hunt. All Superintendent Grimshaw's reserves, official and unofficial, were called into play. The man who was being hunted was Mosley and the message that was to be got to him was that he was to report at once to Dr Godfrey at the cottage hospital. The reason that he could not be found was that he was already there: the last place in the county where anyone would have thought of looking for him.

Earlier on, before it was known that he would be wanted, he had actually been sighted. He had been seen going into a toy shop in one of Bradburn's pedestrianized precincts, where he had made an odd purchase. He had asked first for a

56

construction kit with which unskilled fingers could assemble some species of space vehicle. And when he was told that they were temporarily sold out of such outfits, his disappointment was as keen as a schoolboy's who had been saving up for the thing for weeks. Had they any other playthings to do with space-travel? The girl produced a pocket-size electronic game in whose panel a phalanx of winged marauders could be taken on explosively by a battery of rockets. He played with it for so long that he did not notice that a queue was forming behind him at the counter. He paid for the thing, pocketed it and made his way to the hospital. He was served by a better intelligence network than the one that served Grimshaw.

Dr Godfrey held out a rubber-gloved hand to be shaken. A grey-haired, uncorpulent little man of Mosley's age – though he managed it better – he was wearing a white coat, sparingly spattered with human blood.

'Glad you were able to get here. Are you feeling strong in the stomach? I've got something I want you to look at.'

They were in a consulting-room close to an operating-theatre.

'I want you to look at these before you see the patient. I had some polaroid photographs taken before we cleaned him up.'

Godfrey slid the pictures over to Mosley.

'You wouldn't credit that people expect us to believe the stories they tell us. And we've heard them often enough, we expect them. They have to call an ambulance when things have got out of hand. Then they think up the nature of the accident. Look at these injuries – and we are asked to believe that the young gentleman fell out of a tree.'

The photographs showed weals across the back, the flesh torn over the right shoulder-blade, bruising on both sides of the spinal column, shreds of cotton vest clinging to exudations of congealed blood.

'Two broken ribs. Other lesions that could not possibly have happened on his way out of a tree. No one's going to tell me that this wasn't done with a buckle-belt.'

'Bernard Hunter?'

'You know the folk, do you?'

'I know the family. I've been expecting this.'

'You mean you knew this was likely to happen – and you've let things slide till it has?'

Mosley did not defend himself, simply looked at him with grave, patient eyes.

'I'm sorry, Jack,' Godfrey said. 'I shouldn't have said that. I know what you're up against. Some people need a full-time policeman of their own. But I'll tell you this – and this is why I wanted you here today – this one is going the whole way. I'll have the man who did this in gaol, no matter what that costs the ratepayer. And I'm having no damned clever lawyer playing layman's games with medical evidence. That's happened to me once too often. We need a definitive statement from the lad. He's too frightened to talk. I want you to help me with him – and to be on hand when he does.'

'Won't he admit he was thrashed?'

'Up to now he sticks to his mother's statement: he fell out of a tree he's been forbidden to climb. He's afraid that if he opens his mouth, he'll be thrashed again when he gets home.'

'Surely he won't be in a fit state to talk now?'

'He isn't. But we're going to try. I'm going to break all the rules. We've given him sedatives and pain-killers, and in the normal run of things I wouldn't have a visitor near him. But we'll be cruel to be kind, and I'll give him a knock-out jab when he's said what we want to hear. He'll dream better dreams when he's got it off his chest. He'll come out of shock quicker if he's nothing to wrestle with.'

Bernard Hunter did not look a well child at the best of times. The bed and the hospital paraphernalia seemed to accentuate both his frailty and his pallor. He was lying propped up in the mystery-land between induced sleep and wakefulness – though there was no doubting that he was still conscious. The sight of Mosley reinforced the fear in his eyes. And although he was only nine years old, a degree of artfulness had entered into his soul. Maybe he even had the wits to shelter behind the medications.

'I don't want to die,' he said, and his voice was a pitiful squeak.

So that was what was complicating matters. He knew that the Watlington child had been brought here, found dead on arrival, after the glue-sniffing asphyxiation. Bernard was scared by the thought of a hospital. Georgie Watlington's death had hit him very hard at the time.

'You're not going to die, Bernard,' Godfrey told him, with the right kind of laugh. 'I don't think I've ever had a patient in here who looked less like dying. You're going to feel a bit sore for the next day or two, but we can do something about that. And Mr Mosley has come here because he's your friend. Mr Mosley knows all about you. He knows what happened. He knows the truth. He just wants to hear you tell us about it yourself, then everything's going to be all right.'

The boy opened his eyes and looked directly at Mosley. He could only believe that this was another of the deceptions of the inexplicable adult world.

'I know it wasn't glue-sniffing this time,' Mosley said. 'Or did your father find out about that? Is that why he beat you?'

If he had heard of it, Hunter might well have become violent. His temper was sudden and savage. When beer was swilling about inside him, he was capable of anything. The boy's head moved on his pillow and he closed his eyes.

'Shall I prove to you that I know it wasn't glue this time? I know you'll never do that again. Shall I tell you how much I trust you, Bernard? I went to Skidmore's this morning, as soon as I heard you were in here, and I tried to buy you a space-rocket kit. And those kits, you know, Bernard, they come complete with little tubes of glue. I wasn't frightened of buying it for you. I know I can trust you now to use these things properly.'

Bernard's expression did not change.

'But they had no space-rockets in stock. So I bought you this instead.'

Mosley's hand, already in his pocket, brought out the electronic game. Bernard opened his eyes. Dr Godfrey spoke into his consciousness.

'Look what Mr Mosley has brought you.'

Bernard rested his eyes on the present.

'A few hours from now, you'll be sitting up playing with it.

You'll be taking it to show them at school. And now I want you to tell us why your Mum beat you.'

Bernard's weak face showed impatience with such ignorance. 'It wasn't my Mum.'

'Who was it, then?'

The child fought feebly with inevitability. 'My Dad.'

'And what did he beat you for? Was it the glue?'

'No. You said I wasn't to tell him about the glue.'

'What, then?'

'He said I was telling lies. But they weren't lies.'

'What lies? I'm sure you wouldn't tell lies, Bernard.'

Bernard retreated for a moment as the drugs were taking hold of him. 'Mrs Pearson,' he said at last.

'Mrs Pearson? What about Mrs Pearson? Do you mean old Mrs Pearson or young Mrs Pearson?'

'Mrs Pearson up at the house. I think somebody killed her.' Wide eyes; the consuming fear that only the truly naïve can suffer.

'But nobody killed her, Bernard. We thought somebody might have, but now we've found out where she went.'

It was difficult to see how deeply Bernard was considering this. He did not seem able to follow even such simple reasoning.

'I think my Dad killed her. I *saw* him . . .' The boy swallowed and took a convulsive breath. The effort brought a renewed spasm of pain over the upper half of his body.

Godfrey was beginning to be restive. He put a restraining hand on Mosley's knee. 'We've heard what we want, Jack. Anything else can wait till tomorrow.'

Bernard had started to cry. The ward sister had moved near to the bed and was looking on with concern. Godfrey stood up and mouthed silent words to her, asking her to bring him a hypodermic. Mosley submitted and also stood up.

9

Mosley did not travel up to Hadley Dale on the school bus this time. He demanded transport at the Bradburn station on the grounds that he was bringing in a man who might be violent. Of the two available vehicles, one was out at a by-pass collision, the other scouting for vandals on one of the estates. He was told, reasonably enough, that he could have whichever first became available. But Mosley was not in a reasonable mood. He was as near to being on edge as anyone in the Bradburn nick had ever seen him. He did not seem to want to delay by as much as five minutes his encounter with the Hadley Dale bully. He announced to a stunned outer office that for the first time in his career he was going out on duty in his own private motor: he still used the old-fashioned word.

'Had you better not have someone with you, sir, if he's as dangerous as that?'

'There's Joe Ormerod in the village.'

'Yes, well, I wouldn't want to start mixing it with Joe,' the desk sergeant said. But by then he was talking to himself.

Mosley drove up to the limit. On Stonemill Bank he got behind a sand-lorry and had to fall back hastily to overtake it on a broad bend. Then it suddenly occurred to him that he must have driven through Marrington, though he could not remember having seen the village today, let alone negotiating its bizarre corners. His mind was divided between Ted Hunter and a conversation he had had with Dr Godfrey before leaving the cottage hospital.

Mosley had asked his old friend what he remembered about Matthew Longden from Longden's Bradburn days. Godfrey had looked contemptuous: he was a man who kept his own counsel, and his views on his fellow-citizens rarely coincided with those commonly held.

'A criminal, Jack, if ever there was one.'

'A criminal? You mean doctoring people's books?'

But Godfrey had nothing but scorn for this too.

'A crime to you, Jack Mosley, is something you look up in the statute book. Those aren't the real crimes. The real crimes are against human relationships.'

'And friend Longden?'

'You knew him in those days, Jack.'

'I did, yes, but –'

'Didn't you ever know how he treated his wife? Nothing against the statute book there. Nothing there that isn't done in proper society. But ask anyone who knew her. Or, let's put it another way. Ask any of those who tried to know her – who discovered that she wasn't allowed to be known. Ask Mr Councillor Bootherstone. Ask Colonel Mortimer's wife. Ask the redoubtable Mrs Roffey –'

'Why talk in riddles, Dick?'

'Because I'm sending you to the horse's mouth. You people are always cracking on that you've no room for hearsay. Well – go to those who know . . .'

So Longden had treated Betty badly. Mosley had certainly never suspected it, in the days when he had known both of them. But who was to know what went on in a marriage?

And so he'd tried the same sort of thing on with Lottie Pearson, had he? Anyone less like Betty Longden than Lottie it was hard to imagine. It seemed highly possible that after the initial euphoria things had worn thin between Matthew and Lottie. It was likely that they would. They came from different worlds. Maybe they'd had their rows, and then if one of the television crew had made a pass at her – if she'd found it quite amusing for him to make a pass at her –

The simplest explanation still seemed that Lottie had left voluntarily. But why the repetitions? Why the sand in the porridge? Why the airline tickets in the call-box? And what was he going to be able to get out of Bully Hunter – that young Bernard Hunter already knew?

Mosley was impatient to tread on the accelerator, but again he saw a lorryload ahead, this time of live chickens, obviously destined for Crabtree, up Mallowdale. There would be no hope of getting round that for the next three and a half miles. He cut his losses and turned into a gated road across upper dale farmland. It meant half a dozen stops and starts, assaulting rusted gate fastenings. It played audible havoc with his suspension. But it gave him an illusion of space and decency, even if he hardly ever got out of second gear and his speedometer needle rarely rose above fifteen. There was something to be gained from absorbing the landscape. His mind was rocking between ugly prospects, but the environment remained in perspective: smoke from a farmhouse chimney, the panic of a lamb whose mother had wandered a few yards out of sight, the unpermissive whistle of a man out of temper with his dog.

Mosley drove into Hadley Dale village, and the spectators remained discreetly in the background. Men had been saying all day that he'd be up for Hunter. He looked in the direction of the Hunters' house, as if he were debating whether to call there first. It might help, if he could squeeze a few feckless admissions out of the wife before tackling the man. But Mosley did not go to her. His first call was the police-house – but Joe Ormerod was eight miles away, taking down particulars of a suspected outbreak of sheep-scab. Mosley drove straight on to the quarry, and the manager did not need to be told what he was here for.

'He's working out on the West Scar. Albert Boardman's gang. Shall I have him fetched?'

'You think he'd come?'

It was obviously a relief to the manager that Mosley was going to handle it himself.

'Is it clear to go out there? No red flags up?'

'No firing before half past three. But stick to the track. There's a lot of loose stuff at the edges.'

Mosley made his way from the office-block to an outlying working, amid the thunder of hoppers tipping tons of crushed stone into the kilns. Men in safety helmets watched him pass – but showed no desire to catch his eye. Equivocal was the word for the attitude to authority here. Undoubtedly they would have condemned Hunter without a voice of dissent. They would probably have sent him to Coventry – even at the rock-face, where team-work was vital. But it was a different matter, and no call for applause, when the law came to a work-site. They might co-operate, they might not. It was quite unpredictable.

Mosley came up to where he could see Hunter, working on the flank of a party of eight. He was drilling, boring for the next charge. The foreman came towards Mosley.

'Hunter?'

The movement of Mosley's head scarcely qualified as a nod. The foreman called Hunter's name, an echo against the rock walls. Hunter looked back once over his shoulder, then concentrated on his drill.

'Hunter!'

Men had stopped working. Drills were silenced. A mechanical digger was motionless, a great yellow dinosaur. Only Hunter carried on with his task of the moment, as if his work was all that mattered to him.

'Over here, Hunter!'

Hunter turned off his drill and laid it down, turned slowly and inspected Mosley derisively. The motor of the compressor was rattling on in the background.

'Reckon your chances, do you, Mosley?'

He was red-chested and sweating, the strength of his body insolently challenging under his trousers and shirt. In spite of the warmth of the day, Mosley was still wearing his coat. Hunter began to amble towards him, his boots slithering over shifting rubble. He came within five yards of the detective.

'Not much of you, is there, Mosley?'

'The law's bigger than either of us. And if you have anything else in mind, we'll find room for it on the charge-sheet. You're a big man, Hunter – bigger than a nine-year-old. That's why I've got a warrant for you.'

'Don't come the clever bugger, Mosley.'

Mosley did not move his head. He did not stiffen his posture. The circle of workmen was motionless.

'I've a good mind to teach you a lesson, Mosley.'

'Save your sort of lesson for the younger end.'

A man laughed. That could act as the final goad. Hunter came closer, his uncouth right hand hanging self-consciously loose, as if he were role-playing in a Main Street shoot-out.

'It's up to you, Mosley. Here I am.'

The circle seemed to have come in closer, though no man had

been seen to move. There was no telling what they would do. They had traditional loyalties, and the likes of Mosley ranked low in them. Also, they were of a breed that had not lost the instincts of herd communication. Laughter could unify them. That could be useful to Mosley at this moment.

'What I need is a sling and five stones from the brook,' he said, but that was good for no more than a titter. It was too far removed from their realities.

'You want a stone? Here's one for you.'

Hunter picked up a rock twice the size of his fist and juggled it casually up and down in his hand. Then he retracted his forearm and took aim from his hip.

'Drop it, Hunter!'

The man who spoke was behind Hunter's shoulder, needed only half a step to be within arm's length. Hunter turned his head a fraction and saw that his mates were now hemming him in. Mosley drew handcuffs from his coat pocket and advanced on him with one of them dangling. Hunter stood still while Mosley adjusted the manacle on his wrist.

The foreman ordered the men back to the rock-face. Men from the office and the kilns were standing watching as they walked to the car. Mosley fixed Hunter's wrist to the frame of his passenger seat. Hunter made a sudden attempt to free himself, a massive spasm of strength, hoping perhaps that the metalwork would split asunder. But it held. He must have hurt himself badly, but he showed no sign of that. He sat silent. They had travelled some three or four miles before he spoke.

'How's the boy?'

'Not off the danger-list yet. Whatever happens, you'll answer for it.'

'I didn't hit him that hard.'

'You didn't know how hard you were hitting him. And you didn't care. And you'd no call to be hitting him at all.'

'That kid snivels. There's his like a-plenty on his mother's side.'

'You half kill a lad for a snivel?'

'There was more to it than that.'

'What, then?'

Hunter reflected a long time.

'I'm quick-tempered. The ale does it. I swear I'll stay off it.'

'And how often have you said that?'

Another half-mile of silence. They drove through a cheesy smell of silage. Mosley wound up the window on his side.

'What will I get, Mosley? Does it have to be time? They won't take the kid, will they?'

'That depends on a lot of things. There'll be a lot of people walking all round you: welfare workers, probation officers.'

The thought of it clearly disgusted Hunter. He looked away. They were coming out of Crawdon before he spoke again. Mosley took the hump-back bridge with a good deal more respect for his springs than Ormerod had shown the other night.

'Your word will count for something, won't it, Mosley? I came quietly.'

'What do you expect? A pound from the poor-box for not throwing that stone at me?'

'I've learned my lesson, Mosley, so help me Christ I have.'

'You haven't told me yet what the lad had done to deserve it.'

They were not many miles from Bradburn now. Hunter looked away again.

'I want to piss,' he said presently.

Mosley found a loop of superannuated road that served as a lay-by, unlocked Hunter, let him go up to the hedge without encumbrance. He did what he had to do, came back buttoning his flies.

'You couldn't have stopped me then, Mosley, if I'd had a mind to cut loose.'

'We'd have got you. You'd only have made matters worse for yourself. You don't think I care what they do to you, do you?'

'You might. I could help you, Mosley.'

'That'll be the day.'

'You'd like to know what happened to Lottie Pearson, wouldn't you? The kid's told you all about that, hasn't he – the same as he told his mother.'

'What has the kid told me?'

There had been no further word from the hospital. That was the frustration of frustrations. But he had to leave the timing to Godfrey. Godfrey knew what he wanted the boy's head to be full of.

'You'll have been to see the missus too, I suppose?'

'As a matter of fact, I haven't. I nearly did. Then I thought to myself, I won't put her in the position of having to shop you. I'm giving you your chance to make your statement first. That way it's up to you with her, when you're out and about again.'

Hunter digested this. They were still parked. Mosley had not yet switched his engine on.

'You're not such a bad bugger, are you, Mosley? You're not like some of them. You think about things.'

'The sooner I can stop thinking about you, the better I shall like it.'

'You want to know what happened to Lottie Pearson. I can take you to where her belongings are buried.'

'Where you buried them.'

Hunter turned his face to Mosley.

'That's not all that clever. I suppose the kid told you that. There's no crime in burying old clothes.'

'And where did you bury her?'

'That's where the kid got it wrong. That's why I saw red. Mosley – I'm trying to be straight with you.'

'It doesn't come all that easy, does it?'

Mosley had not put the cuff back on him. Mosley leaned forward to his ignition switch.

'The sooner I've got you indoors, the sooner I can clock off. Unless you care to tell me where I can find Lottie Pearson.'

'She went off somewhere, didn't she?'

'And Matthew Longden paid you to get rid of her things?'

'Not Matthew Longden.'

He seemed to be getting a good deal of satisfaction from putting Mosley right.

'Not Longden. Lottie Pearson herself. She'd been carrying stuff down to one of their sheds, a few at a time. She told me what she wanted done with them. She gave me five quid for it and there'd be another five when she knew I'd made a proper job of it. She said bury them up in the woods. Wrap them up in a blanket. Shape it up like a body. Leave the earth so that anyone could see there'd been digging.'

'What had she in mind? What was she thinking of? All right, so we'd think it was a body. We'd dig it up. We'd find it wasn't a body. That makes no sort of sense to me at all, Hunter.'

This time Mosley did start his engine, crept forward to the exit from the lay-by, waited for an oncoming van and eased them out into the road.

'How the hell do I know what she was thinking of? I only knew what she asked me to do. She was a queer woman, you know.'

'You didn't think to ask her?'

'She wanted to make things awkward for Longden – after what she'd had to put up with from him. And she didn't tell me that. She didn't have to. It stuck out a mile. And she said she'd be back. She was up to something, and I don't know what. And that's God's honest truth, Mosley.'

Mosley chose a series of one-way alleys that led them into the police-station yard without running the curious eyes of the shopping streets. He delivered Hunter at the desk and started on the paper-work.

'Don't forget, Mosley. I've been helpful. Put in a word for me.'

10

Spring was advanced. The sun shone. Clover and ladies'-smocks, dog-daisies and vetches shimmered in the hayfields. Sap rose in oak, ash and alder; leaves and blossoms broke. And if the blood surged afresh in the veins of Mosley's people it did not inspire any increase in the common fund of naughtiness. Yet Mosley, who was normally proud of how rarely he needed to call on the law's retribution, seemed to have started a vendetta against crimes of an unusual – and trivial – nature. Within the space of a week, he submitted more crime reports for the decisions of his superiors than they usually saw from him in the course of a year. There was a comfortless conference between the Assistant Chief Constable and his Detective-Superintendent.

'What's got into Mosley? I've stamped *No Action* on one case-report after another. When does he come up for a routine medical? Ought we to have a quiet word in the MO's ear, do you think? Suggest a spell of mental rest? Might we even breathe the words –' the ACC's eyes sparkled with short-lived hope – 'premature retirement?'

'I fear that Mosley would argue volubly,' Grimshaw said, 'as he has already done in my office. His commission is to seek out and prosecute breaches of the law. It would be illogical to harass him for doing so. That is the innocent line he is taking.'

'But I ask you. He's suggesting a charge against Councillor Bootherstone for *exposing for sale* – how has he expressed it?' The ACC sought the relevant papers. '*Exposing for sale a native leveret in the month of June.*'

'It *is* an offence,' Grimshaw said. 'Under the Hares' Preservation Act of 1892. There is no close season for rabbits and hares, but –'

'Damn it, Grimshaw, I know the law. But it was the Chief's wife he was selling it to. And it wasn't exposed. The carcase had been in his deep freeze since last January. Bootherstone swears it had got lost there. Moreover, Bootherstone is the best friend this force has among elected representatives. *No Action*, Grimshaw, and I'll get my wife to give a dinner-party for the Bootherstones.'

'A wise move, I'm sure, sir.'

'And what's this other thing? Colonel Mortimer, of all people . . .'

Mortimer was President of the Royal British Legion, Chairman of the Borough Justices, Vicar's Warden and a fire-eating reactionary. He believed that the sane world had come to an end with the termination of National Service.

'*Being the person in charge of a captive balloon in flight, leaving it unattended at its moorings.* Has Mosley taken to reading Jules Verne?'

'No, sir. Technically, an offence was committed. Mosley is relying on Article 67 of the Air Navigation Act of 1976 and the subsequent *Regulations.*'

'What has Colonel Mortimer ever had to do with Air Navigation?'

'In the Jubilee Park, sir, last Saturday week. The Colonel was using a captive balloon to draw attention to the forthcoming Church Fête. Actually, Mosley could also have got him for using it to *emit an advertisement or other communication audible or visible from the ground.* He appears to have been missing on that cylinder.'

'That sort of balloon doesn't count. It's only a toy.'

'I fear not, sir. This one fell within the provisions of the order by *exceeding two metres measured in any straight line, including any basket or other equipment attached.* Mosley was scrupulous about measuring it. And it appears that the Colonel had to leave it for two minutes to go and have a pee, thereby contravening –'

'Couldn't Mosley have minded it for him? Wouldn't that have been nearer his conception of the role of a detective-inspector?'

'I haven't fathomed Mosley's inner reasoning on this one yet, sir.'

'Well, I've already told Mortimer that the case will not be proceeded with. But this latest –' the ACC temporarily lost coherence – 'Mrs Roffey . . .'

Someone had once called Mrs Roffey a mixed metaphor: she was at once battle-axe and battle-ship – Past President of the Townswomen's Guild, Major Spoke in the Inner Wheel, Senior District Organizer of the WVS, Marriage Guidance Counsellor and a tower of resource in any community catastrophe.

'*Whilst acting as a street collector for a charity, being accompanied by an animal.*'

'A Flag Day, sir. The Save our Pit-ponies Association. You signed the permit for it yourself. Mrs Roffey was an authorized collector, but was minding a King Charles spaniel for a friend who had gone into Boots. Guide-dogs only, in Boots.'

'And?'

'It's contrary to by-laws, sir.' Grimshaw thumbed the manual. 'Ah, here: *no one to assist without written authority – collectors to be no less than thirty yards apart – no collector to be accompanied by an animal.*'

'How well do you know Mrs Roffey, Tom?'

'Whenever she speaks to me, I stand to attention with my thumbs in line with the seams of my trousers and my feet at an angle of thirty degrees.'

'Go and see her and apologize for Mosley's zeal. And Tom – is Mosley trying to prove something? You don't think he could be an undercover terrorist, do you? A card-carrying Commie? Why has he started this war against the bulwarks of Bradburn society?'

'I wish I could see more clearly what it is he has in mind, sir.'

'Mind? You still cling to your hypothesis that Mosley has a mind? Isn't it the simple truth that he's off his trolley?'

'No, sir. I almost wish that I thought that that was true. I'm afraid that Mosley is being disingenuous. And that has me worried. Of late he has been even more devious than usual – and I wish I knew what he was bloody well up to. It all seems to date from that telex that we had in from Greater Manchester.'

It was a young man who had slipped out again without giving his name who had gone into the police station at Stockport of all places to hand in Lottie Pearson's airline ticket. There had been a very peculiar look on Mosley's face when the message had been passed to him. Somehow, when he had made his meticulous report about finding Lottie's buried belongings, he had made no reference to events in the life of Betty Longden. Certain interesting parallels had not yet been noticed by Grimshaw or the ACC, and Mosley had not yet seen it appropriate to enlighten them. Perhaps he wanted to avoid confusion.

In the meantime, Mosley was showing no signs of impaired mental capacity in the management of his private life. Mosley was an eager amateur cricket umpire at club level, almost pathologically obsessive in his devotion. No call of duty, the scent of no random trails was allowed to interfere with his appointments on the field. On Saturday afternoons he exchanged his raincoat for a garment of starched linen, which he also invariably wore unbuttoned. He even set aside his homburg, always appearing on the greensward in a yellowing old panama. On Saturday afternoons he suffered no worries on the subject of transport: he had no objections to using his own vehicle in the service of cricket. Mosley was what might have been called an umpire's umpire: a solemn guardian of the gravity of the game, an encyclopaedic fountain of its laws; and as inflexible about them as he could show himself about springtime native hares, publicity balloons and unlawfully paraded King Charles spaniels.

On the fourth Sunday in June, Mosley's team, Bradburn Second, was playing away in Hadley Dale, a cherished fixture. Matthew Longden was an active vice-president of the Hadley Dale side, which he financed with a generosity that would have been appreciated on some county grounds. Nothing was ever lacking in equipment or the traditional courtesies. At the height of her tenure, Lottie Pearson had had oversight of the catering, which was enlivened by her often very loud comments on a game of which she had a phenomenal lack of understanding. During her first year as principal tea-maker it had also been necessary – and difficult – to persuade her that players coming into the pavilion steaming from the wicket vastly preferred unimaginative English sandwiches to mountainous flans topped by Alpine summits of whipped cream.

There was very little level ground in Hadley Dale, and the cricket field comprised most of it, though not all of that was flat. There was a notorious falling away in one corner of the deep field.

This afternoon was as near perfect for rural play as an afternoon could be. The climate to which Mosley's people have had to adjust themselves may be a ruthless mould of character, but during ten weeks of the year they can live in reasonable hope of the occasional idyllic day. The smell of freshly mown turf was sweet to the nostril, and the prospect of Bradburn Second's opener seemed unassailable as he widened his shoulders after playing himself in. Douglas Bowers was powerful, if not entirely consistent. He was a mainstay, to be relied on in four matches out of five. Yet he was unpopular, in spite of the matches that he had won for his side – perhaps *because* of them. There was something about his dedication that smacked of the unnatural. For all his fanaticism, he was no cricketer by flair. But he had gone a long way towards making himself one by application. For five years he had been paying for private winter coaching in the indoor nets at Bradcaster, resolute to learn all that was teachable in the way of stroke-play. It was not in the temperament of the rest of his team to find this at all admirable. They did not care for lamp-oil virtuosity. The occasional brilliant failure was greatly preferable.

Distant cattle lowing, the scent of distant hay, a distant cuckoo patrolling the perimeter: all the prime ingredients were there, including Matthew Longden in a deck-chair in the pavilion enclosure and a team of ladies, operating leaderless, but well versed in the construction of the ham sandwich.

Douglas Bowers got his eye in and began to rattle the bowlers' confidence. Two successive attempts to york him devolved into loose balls on the leg side, which went where they deserved to go. Then an accurate, well-pitched ball was less devious than he judged it to be. He tried to knock off non-existent spin, misplaced his feet, and walked into the flight of it. The appeal was highly satisfying to both sides. Bradburn Second would rather lose him than chair him as man of yet another match. Bowers was resigned to his walk back across the green, and looked for the signal from Mosley. Then Mosley spoke an umpire's decision that will be spoken of as long as cricket continues to be played in that part of the country.

'Sorry. Don't know. Wasn't looking. Not out.'

He ought, of course, to have been looking. But as his attention had wandered, and as he had been honest about that, he had no choice but to give the benefit of the doubt to the striker. Bowers carried his bat for 119, for which he received prolonged yet unenthusiastic applause. And there were men who were offhand with Mosley for the remainder of the afternoon. He told none of them what had taken his eye off the ball.

The ACC's dinner-party for Councillor and Mrs Bootherstone was not one of the easier conversation pieces of Bradburn's social year. Tonight, Bootherstone wanted to talk particularly about the marshalling arrangements of the forthcoming Brad

Valley Agricultural Show. It was not easy to divert the talk to the sale of young hares. Yet it was the Councillor who made the final opening for the subject. Like the shock of a gunshot in an empty room, he casually said the name *Mosley*. The ACC jumped visibly in his chair.

'A splendid officer,' Gladwin Bootherstone said. 'A splendid officer. I had occasion to speak with him only the other day – oh, never mind what about: a confidence between us. What your force needs, Assistant Chief, is more officers like him.'

In almost all situations, Tom Grimshaw preferred the approach direct. He called on Mrs Roffey in her Thirties Tudor villa. And at the mention of Mosley, the Amazon actually blushed.

'Now there is a man who is doing four times as much work as he is paid for. I don't mind telling you that only the other week, he rescued me from a situation that could have become vexatious in the extreme. How long is it before he retires, Mr Grimshaw? We must see to organizing a proper public testimonial to him.'

It happened that Mosley had to appear before the Bradburn Bench to give supplementary evidence of arrest in a case brought by a brother officer. The defending solicitor who, being an immigrant from the West Riding, was blunt to local sensitivities, began to treat Mosley with hurtful irony. Colonel Mortimer, not caring how his words might sound if there was an appeal to the divisional court, leaned down from his engine-turned oak throne under the royal coat of arms.

'May I advise you, Mr Digby, that you are listening to evidence from one of this community's most respected officers? He is here today, as always, solely to help this court, and the tone with which you are treating him does nothing to enhance either your credibility or your client's.'

'I don't even have to hear the man's name,' the ACC said. 'I suffer a physical tremor when I even remember his existence.'

There must be some truth in what we were saying the other day. The man is working up to something. And you still have no idea what it is?'

'No. But I cut myself shaving yesterday morning when his name crossed my mind.'

Tom Grimshaw's relations with Mosley were often difficult, but he tried to remain pragmatic. He was, according to the offical break-down of staff duties, in charge of the deployment of Mosley, so there had to be some basis of tolerance between them, even if it stopped short of brotherly love. The ACC, on the other hand, had now abandoned all belief that Mosley might in some way be an asset to his command.

'Do you think that he is aiming at a fundamental disruption of the established order, Tom? I hope you're keeping a close eye on him. Ought we to put someone on his heels? A word with Marsters, perhaps?'

Now Chief Inspector Marsters was Mosley's declared enemy. There was neither pragmatism nor the expiry cf faint hope here. Marsters had no responsibility for Mosley's operational programme. Otherwise he would by now either have suffered a stroke, or in self-defence have developed some grudging liking for the man. As it was, he considered it a personal affront that Mosley should be a member of the same organized body as himself. Veins stood out on Marsters's temples when he was reminded of Mosley.

'I'll have a diplomatic little word with Marsters,' Grimshaw said.

'We'll both have a diplomatic little word with Marsters.'

But as yet there was no one on Mosley's heels to watch how he comported himself when stumps were drawn at the finish of the Hadley Dale match. Douglas Bowers was delighted to get himself into conversation with all and sundry, yet all and sundry seemed adept at avoiding him – except for Matthew Longden, who went over to shake his hand, nobility for ever obliging. In any case, the nature of the offence that Douglas Bowers gave to other cricketers was not something that Matthew Longden could easily have understood.

Mosley did not seem to be in any hurry to leave Hadley Dale. He kept Matthew Longden in sight and attached himself to him as soon as players and spectators were clear of the ground. Longden went round testing that the changing-room doors were locked and began to walk lamely down to where he had parked his car.

'Wait for me, Mr Longden.'

Longden smiled at Mosley's hurrying little legs. 'You don't have to run to catch up with me, Inspector.'

Mosley came up alongside, and as he leaned on his stick, Longden's discomfort seemed pathetically worse for the feeble comedy that he was trying to make of it. They eased themselves down a steep dip to where his car was.

'I need to ask you, Mr Longden, whether Mrs Pearson has made any attempt to get in touch with you.'

'She has not. And if she did –'

'If she did, I take it you would get in touch with us immediately.'

And the odd thing was that it did not look from his expression as if he necessarily would.

'I just wonder if she might try to write to you from Holland.'

'If Holland is where she is.'

'You have reason to doubt that?'

'I would assume that Amsterdam was a stage in her journey to Germany.'

'And Mrs Longden? Do you think that she was also only in Amsterdam in transit?'

Matthew Longden looked as if this whole conversation was so distasteful on his palate that he was going to call an abrupt end to it at any moment.

'I have no way of knowing where my wife went. And I long since ceased to trouble my brain over it.'

'You talked for a long time to our Superintendent Grimshaw, Mr Longden, yet as far as I know you did not mention that there are these capricious similarities between the two cases.'

'*Cases*, Inspector. Everything to you is a *case*. To some of us they seem to be personal catastrophes – until we learn to get over them.'

'I'm sorry I used the word. I think you know me well enough

not to accuse me of being uncaring.'

Longden looked at him without much belief. The shadows of the late spring evening were growing long and tapering, and away at some unmeasured distance they heard the clear-borne progress of a diesel train.

'I know, Inspector. But can't you let this rest, now? Heavens – if you persist in this fashion, you'll end up by bringing her back. And I can't think of anything that would embarrass me more than that would.'

Heavy humour; Mosley did not allow it to put him off course.

'You didn't tell Mr Grimshaw about these similarities,' he persisted.

'I wondered whether to. I decided against it. It could only complicate matters. And these things are wholly irrelevant.'

'You think so? I wonder how you account for them?'

'Account for them? Do I have to account for other people's perversions?'

'They seem strange to an outsider.'

'An outsider, yes – you used the word yourself, Inspector. You didn't live with the woman. No: let me put that less lethally. You didn't have the woman living in your house. So you did not know – at least not at first hand – what vulgarities, what monumental lack of taste she was capable of. You are asking me why history repeats itself – or appears to be repeating itself. It's because it is being made to repeat itself. And it's being made to repeat itself because she knows how to make herself obnoxious. She thinks she's offending me, opening up old wounds.'

'She knew all the details about Mrs Longden's departure, did she?'

Longden shrugged. If he answered that, it would not be because he saw much point in doing so. 'We had talked about it. She was a great one for nosing into things that did not concern her. In the early days, when I first took her on, I made the mistake of being too friendly, too open. I made a rod for my own back, I suppose. Does any of this matter, Inspector?'

Mosley gave no direct answer to that. He went over to a fresh tack. 'When Mrs Longden went away, you leaned heavily on private agencies, if I am not mistaken.'

'That was because your colleagues of that time did not inspire much confidence. They seemed to have made their minds up in advance that she had gone off with a man she had been meeting – and that settled their priorities, once and for all. They did not seem to think that it mattered that I simply did not know where she had gone.'

'And which agencies did you go to?'

'Oh, Lord, I can't remember. I got them out of the yellow pages, two or three of them, one after the other. I might say that I did not let most of them outlast their first verbal report. About all they were good for was keeping a comprehensive account of their alleged expenses.'

'I wish you could remember the name of just one of them,' Mosley said.

Of all the attempts that Longden had made to present a misleading picture, this business of the private detectives was by far the least convincing.

'Why should I remember them? This was all of seven years ago, and if their performance was anything to go by, I would doubt whether a single one of them is still in business. And what are you getting at, Inspector? What are you rooting around for? What are you trying to dig out of a past that's forgotten? There is no aspect of these miserable events that was not gone into by your superior officer, entirely to his satisfaction. And I may say that he is a man in whom I have every confidence, and a gentleman of a vanishing breed. Now I would hate to have to go to him and complain to him of harassment –'

'I'm sorry you should feel that there's anything like that,' Mosley said mildly. 'My commission is simply to arrive at the truth.'

'And you do not think I have been telling it, is that it?' Longden was over the top now and out from cover with bayonet fixed.

'The passage of time sometimes dulls our memories in spite of ourselves,' Mosley answered, his tone sadly apologetic.

'Meaning what, Inspector? If you think that I have anything to gain from misleading you –'

'Nothing is farther from my mind. But if I could just ask one more question –'

'What's that? I'll answer it if I think you have the right to be asking.'

'I just wonder whether there have been any other parallels between these two ladies, other than this coincidence of the airline tickets.'

Chance for him, at any rate, to say something about the sand-believed-arsenic. But Longden threw away the opportunity to clear himself.

'There have not. How could there be? And I resent the insinuation that I am open to question. I refuse to answer anything further except to your Superintendent Grimshaw. I shall ring him forthwith and complain of your attitude. I do not propose to have myself pin-pricked by a junior officer.'

'In that case, I'll wish you good day, Mr Longden. I do hope that if you happen to remember the names of any of those enquiry agents, you will get in touch.'

A sweet smell of evening. Mosley passed a farm of which even the coarser yard odours seemed like a healthy reminder of a clean and uncomplicated past. He went to call on Joe Ormerod at the police-house. Joe was sitting down to his Saturday-afternoon high tea of brown bread and cockles, his wife having returned on the bus from her shopping. At various points in the room there were specimens of a new generation of Omerods, one of whom, a boy of nine or ten, bore so close a facial resemblance to his father as to look like some kind of family joke.

There was this to be said for PC Ormerod: he was not as dense-witted as he looked. Not quite. If that had been the case, society would surely have found some sort of refuge for him; he would certainly not have been allowed to play any acknowledged role in keeping society in order. His eyes and brow seemed combined in a permanent frown at his inability to understand the things about him. His narrow forehead, not dissimilar to that of *theropithecus gelada*, the Gelada baboon, suggested that here was a creature to whom epistemology and causation came as something of a puzzle. But Mosley knew that Joe Ormerod sometimes noticed things, though it did not always occur to him to pass them on. Joe's favourite conversational tactic was silent withdrawal. His general attitude to trouble was one of non-interference. He had learned from experience that this sometimes encouraged difficulties to find their own solution. But he could also accumulate seams of arcane knowledge, and with patience and skill, these pockets of crude ore could sometimes be tapped.

The Ormerods were drinking tea from cups that each contained three-quarters of a pint. One of the most striking objects on the table was a tea-pot well capable of servicing such a battery of vessels. Joe's wife poured a cup for Mosley.

'When did you last see Jack Pearson in Hadley Dale, Joe?'

'Not since he left,' Joe said, a characteristic Ormerod answer, but one which was perfectly satisfactory to Mosley. 'Not since they saw him off,' Joe added. 'The pair of them walked either side of him to the parish boundary.' That was a story that Mosley already knew.

'He was here this afternoon,' Mosley said. 'Came up to the cricket field while Doug Bowers was batting. Didn't show himself in the open though. Came slinking up along that dead ground behind deep extra cover.'

Joe washed down a prodigious aggregate of wholemeal bread and masticated molluscs, then swilled away this obstacle to speech.

'Oh, aye?'

'And I'll tell you what, Joe, I got so tied up in it, I had to give Bowers not out. Matthew Longden spotted him the same moment I did. Got up out of his deck-chair and went hobbling round the back, casually, you know, as if he were going to the gents. Two or three minutes later I saw the pair of them together behind the score-box, down in that gully where they wouldn't be seen from the benches. And that had me wondering.'

Perhaps Ormerod considered it presumptuous to anticipate a superior's question. He did not react in any way.

'What has Longden ever had to do with Jack Pearson?'

Ormerod speared with his fork the best-fed cockle on his plate. 'Used to work for him,' he said. 'When Longden first came up here. Odd jobs. Clearing rubbish behind the house. Sawing logs. Window cleaning. Didn't last long, though. Bit too much like earning his keep, for Jack Pearson, I reckon.

Longden gave him his cards and Ted Hunter took over.'

'When, Joe, when? How long did it last? A week, a month, two months?'

Joe knitted his brow – not an achievement on which outside observers would have staked much betting money. 'Let me see, now. It was Jack Pearson who shovelled the winter coals in, but I think it was Ted Hunter who did the snow-ridding when we had that big fall.'

'What I'm trying to get at, Joe –'

There were times when you had to ask Joe leading questions if you were to keep his mind on the subject at all.

'What I'm trying to get at, is: which of them, Pearson or Hunter, was odd-job man at the time Mrs Longden went her ways?'

'Jack Pearson,' Ormerod said, without hesitation. 'I know, because there'd been a hell of a to-do. Mrs Longden had said something sharpish to Jack, like, and old Matthew was supposed to have come across him loosening the nuts on the car-wheels.'

'Eh?'

'That's how it was,' Ormerod said.

'But surely Longden would have got rid of him there and then.'

'It wasn't long after.'

'But on the spot, Joe.'

Ormerod clearly was applying his mind to the anomalies behind this. 'I never did think we'd heard the whole story,' he said.

'The fact remains that the moment Jack Pearson appears on the edge of the cricket field, Matthew Longden gets up and goes to him. Keeps him out of sight and stands talking to him for six or seven minutes. Making me miss giving Bowers leg before. There's something going on in this village, Joe.'

'I wouldn't be sur-wondered.'

This was by a wide margin Ormerod's favourite verbal joke, and one that he aired at some point during most conversations with him.

'I want to know everything – *everything* that happens up here in the next week or two.'

Joe nodded his promise and then hastened to pass on something that he already knew. 'I suppose you know that that lot are coming up here again.'

'No, I didn't. What lot?'

'That television lot. They're making another film.'

And this was news to Mosley.

'Aye. End of summer. Going to be about a dragon. Up in Kestrel Clough. All fixed up with Isaac Oldham, because Longden wouldn't have them on his premises again. They've booked up every room in the Plough. Every bed and breakfast that's to be had in Hadley.'

'Oh, aye?'

'Up Kestrel Clough. Night time. Making a new film. Been to see Isaac Oldham to make arrangements for the dragon. Going to be a real dragon. Isaac Oldham's going to have to feed it.'

There ought to be some grist for Tom Appleyard and Brad Oldroyd in those goings-on.

'Same people, you say, Joe?'

'Aye. And some say it was one of them that Lottie Pearson went off with. So we're waiting to see.'

He was waiting to see. Hadley Dale was waiting to see. A dragon up Kestrel Clough. Ellerman Tovey interviewing them while Tom Grimshaw and the ACC sat by their sets. A man on the production team who still might have Lottie Pearson in tow.

Joe Ormerod wiped up briny cockle-juice with a corner of crust.

'There's one more thing while I'm here, Joe. What's the feeling about Hunter?'

'Folks don't think it's right,' Ormerod said.

An answer that he seemed to think was self-explanatory. Mosley gave him time to expand.

'What do they think's not right, Joe? Whose side is the village on?'

'Hunter's,' Joe said. 'Shouldn't have hit the kid like he did, but hasn't done him any lasting harm. But he shouldn't have to be fighting to get his own lad back. Well, I ask you – should he?'

'What if he's going to whale the daylight out of him again?'

'He won't,' Joe said with certainty. 'Hunter's had a shake-up. He's off the ale.'

The case was still on remand. Hunter was out on bail. It was coming up for disposal in a week or two, after social and medical reports. The opinion of Hadley Dale was interesting. People made mistakes from time to time, up in the cloughs and fells, but if they had reached the stage of forgiving Hunter, they must have their reasons for it.

'He's not set foot in the pub since,' Joe said.

'He's tried that before in his time. It's never lasted all that long.'

'If they take the kid off him, he'll go out of his mind.'

'And what about the kid's mind?'

'I think, personally, meself,' Joe said, 'they ought to give him his chance. Hunter's missus has bought herself a new coat with one week's beer savings.'

'Nothing will convince me that the man is not a stark, staring lunatic.'

Chief Inspector Marsters had come back to the ACC and Tom Grimshaw with his carefully considered findings about Mosley's activities. The experience seemed to have brought him a stage nearer to his point of apopletic no-return. The purplish mesh above his cheek-bones was now positively incandescent and his temporal veins were knotted and throbbing. Any statement by Marsters on Mosley was certain to be vicious. But he rarely had the luxury of being commissioned to make one. And it was animal savagery that these two wanted to hear: especially since the hard work that Grimshaw had had to put in on the phone to Matthew Longden.

'Mind you, he's not the only one in this town who seems to be going round the bend. You remember he wanted to bring charges against Councillor Bootherstone and Mrs Roffey?'

'We do. If you recall, that was the reason why we asked you to –'

'Anyone would think to hear them talk that Mosley was doing them a favour. You'd think that some extract of violets was puffing out of Mosley's arse. Mrs Roffey is even trying to work out that he has chances of promotion.'

'Yes,' the ACC said. 'We are aware that in some men's

vision, Mosley's eyes have a bluish tinge just now.'

'He seems to have ingratiated himself with these people. If you ask me, he has used these ridiculous charges for some purpose of his own.'

'We have gathered that. What we wanted to know –'

But Marsters could only say what was filling his own head.

'It seems that he went along to each of them in turn, homburg in hand, apologizing profusely and saying that some common informer, whom he refused to name, had been laying informations against them. About captive balloons, flag-days, hares in the deep freeze. They would understand, wouldn't they, that he only had his duty to do.' Marsters went into a mincing tone that was totally unjust either to Mosley or any of the principals. 'They would understand that he could not stop the papers going forward. But they could rest assured that nothing would come of any of these ridiculous charges. They could trust Mosley to handle them discreetly behind the scenes. He would see to it personally that they all went into the shredder.'

'*Mosley* would see to that?'

'So that's why they think the world of him, those three. If you ask me, Mosley's up to something.'

'If you remember,' the ACC said, 'so do we. We asked you to find out what. And while you're here, there's another thing –'

There seemed to be a lot of bile brimming over in top offices this morning. Marsters had not expected that any of it would be coming his way.

'It's now thirteen weeks since we had the first complaint about quick-snatch housebreakings on your patch. Two or three every week, regular. And we seem to have missed the echo of cell-doors slamming. *Digito extracto*, Marsters. Or we shall have to pass the case-file on to Mosley.'

11

Mosley crossed the road from Joe Ormerod's to Sarah Pearson's. Sarah Pearson had settled down to her Saturday evening's indulgence. She had washed up her tea-things, and they were standing on her scrubbed but rotting wooden draining-board and she was sitting in a fireside chair listening to a programme of radio comedy – or such of it as was not obscured by static. A modest glass of grocer's port stood on a stool within easy reach of her hand. She waved Mosley to her other chair.

'What was he after?' Mosley asked her.

'What was who after?'

'Your Jack.'

'Nay. I don't know what you're talking about.'

Mosley let his eyes scan Sarah Pearson's scanty possessions. She had been sly. If she had offered her son tea, she had put his cup and saucer away, and there was only crockery for one at the side of the sink. But someone had brought her a Bradcaster midday paper which she had not thrown away, no doubt promising herself a rare hour of local tittle-tattle. And at the back of her fire he spied a cigarette-end that had so far escaped flame and embers: Sarah Pearson did not smoke.

Mosley let her see where his eyes were travelling, and she did not shirk the obvious conclusions. She had a sharper brain than Joe Ormerod, and knew when a battle was lost in advance.

'Is it a crime nowadays, then, for a mother to mash tea for her son?'

'Far from it,' Mosley said. 'I'm always glad to see the end of any civil war.'

'Oh, aye?'

The commonest two syllables in the Dale, into which intonation could inject a rich variety of meanings. In this instance, Sarah Pearson was making a statement of her irreparable disbelief.

'I knew he'd come back,' Mosley said. 'Oh, it's the tale of the Dale that the pair of you saw him off. But he wouldn't want his poor old Mum to be fending for herself, now, would he?'

'You're a clever bugger,' she said.

'And so are you. Clever enough to see what's going to come next.'

'Oh, aye?'

Now the meaning was that she rejected this sort of soft-soap talk – but that she wanted to know where he was leading her.

'Coming back to live with you, is he?'

'That's as may be.'

'He couldn't stand living with his wife, because she saw right through him, and couldn't keep her tongue quiet for a minute about what she saw. You know how to get a message to him?'

'Why should I want to do that?'

'So that you can pass him a message from me.'

'Oh, aye?'

Meaning that he could talk as much as he liked and she would hear the message first, before she decided whether to pass it or not.

'Tell him there's no future in trying to get money out of Matthew Longden. He may find himself in bigger trouble than he's ever struck yet.'

She looked as if she did not believe this. To admit that she did would come close to admitting that she knew what her son was scheming.

'Tell him we know where Lottie's belongings were laid to rest.'

'You think you kept that dark? Every silly bugger in the village knows about that.'

The studio audience laughed at some gag of the radio comics. Mosley went over and switched off the set. Neither of them was listening to the programme, but both of them knew that his action was an unpardonable liberty to take in a stranger's house.

'Listen, Sarah –'

And that was a greater liberty still. The use of Christian names in the Dale was governed by a code that bristled with significance.

'Tell him I want to know where he buried Betty Longden's tackle. And if I happen to find out before he tells me, I shall not be on his side.'

Sarah Pearson held her eyes fixed on Mosley's face. To agree to what he was asking might be tantamount to all manner of admissions. But she had known Mosley, in one context or another, for many years.

'I'll think about it,' she said.

The next day was Sunday, and Joe Ormerod rang Mosley halfway through the morning. 'You wanted to know everything that happened up here. Anything unusual, you said.'

'That's right, Joe.'

'Sarah Pearson was out in her Sunday best before eight this morning. Round at Sam Parkinson's garage, wanting to know what he'd ask to run her into Bradcaster. I don't know how much she paid him. She has a few quid put by, you know. But as soon as he'd had his breakfast, he drove her out in that big black Austin that he uses for funerals.'

In the course of the next few days, Marsters made frequent short reports on Mosley's activities.

He seemed to be spending an inordinate ration of his time on the case of that battered boy. Surely, as far as the CID was concerned, all the paper-work on that should have been finished weeks ago? It was for the Halo Squad now, the welfare and county care people, to be putting their spanners in the wheels of justice. Did Mosley think he was being paid to do their work for them?

Then he had spent an hour one morning in Raven's furniture shop, talking to Ernest Weatherhead in the back office between customers. Why Ernest Weatherhead? Weatherhead could not possibly be an informant on anything that interested Mosley. Weatherhead did not stir out of the inside shadows of the shop for long enough to have any information about anything.

Marsters felt a heightened glow of excitement. A few more reports like this, and Mosley would be booked for a medical board. They'd find clear evidence of brain deterioration.

Then the mystery deepened. Mosley applied for two days of

his annual leave, tacked them on to a rest day and disappeared into the unknown. Marsters was unable to account for him to the D-S and the ACC. But on his return, Mosley picked up his phone and rang Chief Inspector Marsters in the headquarters office.

'Just to apologize. You must have been wondering where I've been.'

'What the hell do you mean?'

'I wouldn't like you to think I've been trying to give you the slip.'

'I don't know what the blazes you're talking about.'

'I know my movements interest you. I've only been to Bradcaster. Stayed at one of the smaller commercials. I thought I'd better let you know that I'm back.'

He put down the phone after hearing what appeared to be a visceral implosion. Then he went for a quiet walk in the Jubilee Park, leaned on the balustrade of the bridge and looked down at the ducks. There was a superfluity of drakes in this pond, which led to random and colourful activity. A background of random activity somehow always helped Mosley to reflect.

He had spent a busy time in Bradcaster. He was not a big city man, and was always liable to misjudge distances when he was in one. He rarely thought it necessary to take to public transport and consequently did a great deal of trudging about long streets.

If Matthew Longden had been able to find what he wanted in the yellow pages, then so could Mosley. He argued that Longden would never have used the only private eye in Bradburn. For one thing he was too well known, and, for another, so was his inefficiency. But he wouldn't have gone further afield than Bradcaster: local flavour was too important. Mosley was lucky to find an issue of the directory for the year in which Betty Longden had gone, so he was able to save the waste of time spent on firms that had opened since. He arrived at a short list of six, of whom two had gone out of business and one had died. The first in whose office he actually found himself was a retired detective-sergeant from the Sheffield force, a man called Colley, who had a heavy cold – and no inhibitions whatever about discussing a previous client's business. He seemed conversation-starved, and took great pleasure in talking to a serving policeman. Perhaps he had his eye on reciprocal favours for the future.

It took him a little time, however, to remember Longden. Then he had recourse to a bulging filing system, which he had obviously never weeded since he had opened his bureau. He cursed as he crushed his knuckles getting them in and out of the tightly concertinaed folders, and in the end it was mostly from human rather than paper memory that he talked.

'I remember the bugger. Bad-tempered cow-son. Wanted results in half a day, and queried the price of a cup of coffee when I'd gone without my lunch. Paid up, though: on the nail.'

Colley lit a cigarette that rasped his inflamed membranes, and had a coughing fit into a paper tissue.

'To tell you the truth, though, I ended up wondering whether he was bloody interested. I made a preliminary report to him by telephone, which was what he had asked me for. But he cut me off short. I don't think he even listened to what I was trying to tell him. He told me I was taken off the case before he'd heard half of what he'd asked me to find out. I couldn't care less. There wasn't much in it for me, and it wasn't interesting. Just one of those cases where the woman had obviously beetled off because she couldn't stand him a minute longer. And if the way he treated her was anything like the way he treated me, I don't know how she'd stuck him as long as she did. Of course, I know he was upset. He's not the only one by a long chalk I've seen in that condition. They always seem to blame the next bugger they meet for all that's happened to them.'

Colley coughed again and took a pastille from a tin on his desk.

'And what did you find out that he wouldn't let you tell him?' Mosley asked.

'Well, I'd traced her to Bradcaster railway station and on to the London express. But I honestly don't think he heard me tell him that. He started bellyaching about paying through the nose for the obvious before I'd finished what I was saying.'

'The *London* express?'

'Oh, aye. I watched her get aboard with my own eyes. And she'd queued at the office for a reservation.'

89

'You're sure you were following the right woman?'

Colley laughed. 'I can see you're a man of some experience. He'd lent me a photograph. He was so keen to get it back that I could picture him drooling over it for the rest of his days. I snapped a copy of it, because I'd a partner in those days who shared the watching with me. I dare say I've still got it.'

He plunged his fingers again in amongst the tightly wedged folders, and came out with a snapshot that he passed to Mosley. Mosley did not know the woman in a summer print frock of the 1950s who had been caught by a beach photographer on the promenade at Morecambe.

It was certainly not Betty Longden.

Mosley's next call was on Paterson, Rudge & Stevenson, a one-man firm run by a man called Watts, whose qualification as a private investigator was a failed law degree. He probably picked up enough dubious work from Bradcaster solicitors to make an income. Some of his more lucrative clients might well be impressed by his public-school drawl and by his hint of cynical disregard for any professional except himself.

He staunchly refused to discuss any man's affairs with Mosley, putting on an act of outraged etiquette at any such monstrous suggestion. Mosley sat for a moment silent, almost as if he had not heard any of this; or, at least, as if he were about to produce some surprise in the way of a bargaining counter. His trousers were baggy at the knees, and his shoes, never very highly buffed, were whitened by the dust of the Bradcaster pavements. Watts looked as if he were measured for a new suit every two weeks or so, and threw all his neckties away after a single wearing.

Then Mosley stood up, conveyed a non-verbal apology and made his way through the outer office. There had been a time somewhere in the middle of his life when he had learned what kind of encounter not to waste time and effort on.

And so to the last of his hopes.

Houston was a man with a thick Glaswegian accent that had not responded to a working lifetime in Bradcaster. He was a busy man whose telephone frustrated continuous conversation every two minutes or so, and who seemed to have several hundred irons simultaneously in the fire, of which he was in command of the detail without having to remind himself. He was also extremely and candidly suspicious, and gave the impression of being so hard-bittenly astute that he must have spent a long career anticipating attempts to outwit him. Yet he did not dismiss Mosley out of hand. Where there were chances, Houston explored them.

'You say you work the Bradburn area?'

'Bradburn Rural.'

'That includes Marrington? Stonemill?'

'Place-names etched on the lining of my heart.'

'Does the name Garrod mean anything to you?'

'Edwina Garrod?'

'The same.'

Mosley winced in exaggerated fashion.

'Not to be taken at her face value?' Houston asked.

'Or her apparent cash value either,' Mosley said.

Houston wrote something on a jotter.

'Obliged. Now what can I do for you?'

Houston listened, and did not pretend to remember Matthew Longden or any assignment for him.

'But I don't clutter my mind with what's gone before. If I ever did anything for him, it'll be in the records. Give me approximate dates, and I'll go through the books. Can you call back tomorrow morning?'

The outcome was that Houston told how he had been engaged by Longden some weeks before the disappearance of his wife. His task had been to find the identity of the man whom she had been meeting in Bradcaster on the sly. What had happened was that she had had a series of dental appointments, for root-canal work, on Thursday afternoons. There were greener-over-the-hill reasons why she had not had it done in Bradburn. She always came into the city by bus because Longden needed the car, and he could not run her over himself because Thursday was his Rotary day. The service time-tables were wretchedly unhelpful and condemned her to a weekly wait of some two and a half hours during which she started taking a leisurely tea upstairs in Marley's. The word was not slow in reaching Hadley Dale that it had become a weekly event for her to share a table in a discreet corner of the restaurant. It never did become clear who had actually seen them, but there was a confident consensus description of the man: perhaps five, even ten years younger than her, well dressed, quietly spoken and carrying an executive brief-case that suggested an established vocation. It was thought, from the tender, even proud way in which he looked at her, that he must be becoming very fond of her indeed, and they must have something on their consciences, because they were always careful not to be seen coming out of the restaurant together.

Then a further report went the rounds – brought by Mrs Wilson, a dormitory migrant to the village, who had been taking her child to town for expensive orthodontic consultations. The new story was that Mrs Longden had not been to the dentist at all that afternoon, and had not been expected there. Nevertheless, she had travelled in on the bus as usual.

'I remember it all now,' Houston said. 'Longden was a very bitter man, very angry because I couldn't tell him what he wanted to hear. I'd been to the cafe, ye ken, I'd talked to the waitresses, I'd had a word with other regular customers. I'd also talked to yon dentist's wee receptionist, and I'd come to the conclusion that there was nae man.'

'But there had been dental appointments?'

'In the first instance. But the visits to Bradcaster had gone on long after her treatment was complete.'

Mosley leaned on the balustrade and waited for a moorhen to reappear after a long expedition down among the bottom weeds.

Dick Godfrey had given him the names of three people who knew more about Betty Longden than they had ever told. He had already done the spadework on them.

12

When the dust had all finally cleared – when the linen, as it were, was fluttering like bunting on the line – there were some not altogether unsympathetic inquests behind the scenes on the manner in which Mosley had conducted himself. The opinion was strongly held that he had taken a quite unnecessarily circuitous route to soften up his eminent informants, that he had been elaborately devious simply for his own amusement. Mosley was not given to justifying himself. When opinions were being expressed that were obtusely critical of his methods, his habit was to receive them in silence and absent himself about fresh work at the first opportunity. But he had been heard to mention to a colleague how he had come to act as he did with Councillor Bootherstone, Colonel Mortimer and Mrs Roffey.

'Not easy bodies to manipulate, that lot. Not much imagination for problems other than their own, and very ready to defend those they consider belong to their own kind. If, on the other hand, you can somehow get them into your debt – like saving them from a dollop of aggro – Colonel Mortimer wouldn't have wanted to appear before neighbouring justices, so that fair play could be seen. Mrs Roffey could have gone on collecting for flag-days, but she might never have been chairman again. Councillor Bootherstone would have to have paid a nominal fine, because he *had* committed a technical offence. And I was the one who had pulled them out of all that. So when I called . . .'

He did not feel at ease, calling on Mrs Roffey. But then, where did he feel at ease? For what occasion could his everyday clothes fit him, except perhaps for a society of unemployed pigeon-fanciers at the funeral of one of their friends? When he was visiting Mrs Roffey, he even felt incapable of sitting properly on a chair. His stubby fingers looked, he knew, as if he could not move one of them without moving them all. He held

Mrs Roffey's bone china cup as if he were afraid that the delicate handle might spontaneously detach itself. And Mrs Roffey, watching uneasily from her cushions, looked as if the same thought might be running through her mind too.

Mrs Roffey's drawing-room was the showcase of the most influential woman in Bradburn. She was the only woman in the town to possess a grand piano. It always stood open, and the same piece of music was always open at the same page on its rack: something in five flats that leaped about a mountain-range of semi-quaver arpeggios. No one had ever heard her play a note.

Somewhere in the background of her happiest of possible marriages there was a Mr Roffey whose business, the reconstitution of textiles from rags, shreds and waste, kept him for the most part absent from home. The word *shoddy* was not one which Mrs Roffey could ever bring herself to use of the basis of her financial security.

She was demonstratively happy to see Mosley again, especially since he was able to open by assuring her that the affair of the lawless King Charles spaniel had now indeed been consigned to the salvage. When he brought up the name of the former Bradburn accountant, she had necessarily to launch herself on a powerful moral diatribe.

'Quite disgusting. Quite disgusting. If he finds himself now left alone in that cold old barracks at his age, he has only himself to thank for it. And the way he comported himself with that German woman! I mean, I have nothing against Germans as Germans, but when all's said and done, they are Germans. Even in Teape's, at the bacon-counter, you could see the lust fairly oozing out of her eyes. You know what my husband said about him: third mate to a German destroyer.'

She laughed in a manner that activated every unsupported ounce of her flesh. Mosley smiled coyly. He forebore to wonder aloud that her husband had ever remained at home long enough to formulate such a gem.

'So different from Mrs Longden,' Mosley said.

'Ah!'

For a moment it quite looked as if she had recognized an attempt to decoy her into a betrayal of confidences. It would have come as no surprise if she had then said that, alas, this was not a subject to be discussed by charitable society. But the second time she said, 'Ah!' she shook her head knowingly.

'So charming. So sweet-natured. So uncomplaining. And so *repressed*. She had money, you know – but of course a good deal of it went into the business. Those new premises in Cross Street: I never saw the necessity for them. And he was so *jealous*. He couldn't bear for her even to talk to a man. I believe there was even a row over that weedy little Weatherhead in Raven's. And he wouldn't let her do things. You'd have thought, wouldn't you, that a man in his position would have wanted her to be a corner-stone in everything that went on in the town. If there was a chance that she might exchange two words with a member of the male sex, then he forbade it. Do you know that she never once took part in a charitable activity? Not even Haig's poppies? And do you know what he had the nerve to say to her, when she plucked up the nerve to ask if she might? He told her he could not bear the thought of her loitering in shop doorways. My God, I'd like to see my husband try to keep me out of shop doorways.'

If Mosley's imagination extended to an image of Mrs Roffey on the game, he succeeded in suppressing it.

'No, the trouble with Matthew Longden was that he was first, foremost and finally a book-keeping man. Double-entry ledgering had entered into his soul. He wasn't capable of being married to a woman. He co-habited, Mr Mosley, with something that had to be seen to balance. He had to assure himself at intervals that her assets exceeded her liabilities. Do you know that they had a dreadful scene on the first Monday night of each month when he went over her housekeeping books? She had to keep all her receipts. I remember once she picked up a W.H. Smith check-out slip on the pavement, and said it might come in useful if she had some item unaccounted for. It wasn't that money was ever tight in the house, you know. It wasn't even that he was mean: I'll go so far as to say he could be generous to a fault. But everything had to be *right*.'

'I'm surprised that she tolerated it for so long,' Mosley hazarded.

'Well, she didn't, did she? She went kicking over the traces in

Bradcaster, didn't she? But I'll never believe that there was any man involved in that. I think she went to a lot of trouble to cover up for what she was getting up to in Bradcaster. But it was not for a man. That I simply won't have. If you ask me, she went to all those lengths just for the sake of a quiet cup of tea once a week.'

Then Mosley went to see the Bootherstones at home, and that was a dialogue that needed a somewhat different approach. Councillor Bootherstone and his wife were a couple for whom there was no greater attainable heaven on earth than their own uneventful, uncoloured, unventuresome, unquestioned family life. They had been married forty-five years. They never contradicted each other. They never even had to discuss which television channel to watch. And the only people of whom they truly approved lived, they assumed, in a similarly static domestic paradise. Yet when it came to discussing the Longdens, there was something that was possibly shrewd about their diagnosis.

'You know, we were always very fond of both of them. What happened – well, it came as a very great surprise to us. I mean, Matthew had done my books ever since the pair of us started in business.'

Could there be any safer guarantee of marital integrity than that?

'There were times, though, when I was tempted to take Matthew on one side and warn him. It had come as a surprise to us when we learned that he was marrying a woman from away. Oh, and she was a beauty, but very reserved, you know. Perhaps that did not go down too well in Bradburn. And they seemed so close together – as, indeed, they *were* close together. But Matthew had old-fashioned ideas. I'm not saying he clung to the ancient view that a man's wife belongs to a man, goods, chattels and all. But there were times when he behaved as if that's what he thought. He still believed in the obedience clause.'

'I'm surprised that she tolerated it so long,' Mosley said, not for the first time that day.

'But then she loved him. And it took time to get used to him. And when you get used to things, you don't want to change.'

'And her vows were made in front of an altar,' Mrs Bootherstone said. 'There are people to whom such things matter, you know, Mr Mosley. I remember she said to me, "My vows were made at the altar. Or else –" '

'*Or else* – well, it came to *or else*, didn't it?'

'That's something we've never believed, Mr Mosley. That's something we've never let our minds dwell on. That a respectable married woman should be making assignations upstairs in Marley's . . .'

As Mosley was ready to go, Bootherstone gingerly brought up his own criminal record.

'That business about my deep freeze, Inspector –?'

'Oh, you can forget about that,' Mosley said. 'There were one or two voices at headquarters that went on demanding blood for a day or two, but I managed to talk them out of it in the end.'

When he was asked for opinions, as man to man, Colonel Mortimer generally assumed that all men's outlooks were as his was, and he often wrapped up his answers in a coarseness that one would never have guessed from his deportment on the magisterial bench. It was a promising portent when that happened, the offer of a Shibboleth that he was on your side. He thought for a few seconds when Mosley brought up the inside story of Betty Longden.

'I remember an old Major, second-in-command at the Depot, who had a recipe for holding on to a woman. Keep her well-fed, he used to say, well-shagged and ill-shod. It always seemed to me that Matt Longden must have come unstuck somewhere. She bought her shoes at Carruthers, and she never looked hungry to me, so – of course, no man knows what goes on in another man's bed, but when I saw them out together, it sometimes crossed my mind to wonder whether he was doing her justice. I reckon he was under-estimating her need for it, but you can't go about telling a fellow that, can you? Not in civilian life, anyway. And yet, from what I've heard of his carryings-on this last year or two, he seems to have been open to further training, the crafty old bugger. This fellow Hunter comes up the day after tomorrow, by the way. What are we going to do about him?'

A supplementary picture emerged with the help of Ernest Weatherhead, though when it came to opinions, Mosley had to tease them from him.

As Chief Inspector Marsters had reported, Mosley seemed to be spending a lot of his time in the office at the back of the furniture shop, amid carpet patterns, upholstery samples and bees'-wax polish. Roderick Raven these days was not spending in aggregate much more than half an hour a day on his premises.

Ernest Weatherhead was repeating his familiar complaint about Matthew Longden, who never let him forget his single lapse from honesty. Mosley was listening as closely as if he were hearing it for the first time.

'So you became quite a regular visitor to his home?' Mosley said.

'Not exactly frequent. It all started when I paid him the last instalment of what I owed him. He said we must celebrate that. I must bring Margaret round to supper at his house.'

'Was that the first time you had met Mrs Longden?'

'I had seen her about town, knew who she was. She had been in the shop once or twice, always knew precisely what she wanted, wouldn't have substitutes. Some of the locals called her toffee-nosed, but they'll say that of anyone who doesn't speak with a Bradburn accent.'

'You didn't find her toffee-nosed at supper?'

'Far from it: delighted to have us. And Margaret will tell you the same thing. She and Mrs Longden got on like childhood pals. We invited them back to a meal at our house: but they didn't come. It was obvious they didn't want to. It was a relief in a way. We hadn't much room in those days.'

'Had you the feeling that if it had been left to Mrs Longden alone, they would have come?'

'I couldn't say, Mr Mosley.'

A barrier? An unwillingness even to think about the question?

'But you yourself did pay other visits to the Longden household?'

'Sometimes. Sometimes Mr Longden had an audit at a stage that was purely mechanical. I'd do the arithmetic for him.'

'For a fee?'

'Mrs Longden always brought me a nice supper tray.'

'Good Heavens! Look at the time! And I'm supposed to be meeting one of my sergeants on the other side of town.'

Mosley hurried out of the shop. In the afternoon, not more than five minutes after the OPEN/CLOSED notice on the door-pane had been turned round again, he was back.

'I don't want you to think I am persecuting you, Ernest. But I've been thinking of some of the things you told me this morning.'

Weatherhead was a desperately overworked man, and he was beginning to be worried about the devastation of his time.

'When Mr Longden moved over to Hadley Dale, did you continue to do work for him at his home?'

'Not very often, Mr Mosley. He had retired. Perhaps he'd still do a tax-return for a friend, or cast his eye over charity books.'

'So he did ask you over sometimes?'

'Sometimes.'

'Whose books? Which books was he still doing?'

'I'm trying to remember. Mr Bootherstone's for one. The Hadley Dale Community Centre Fund.'

'Did you notice any change in the Longdens' life-style?'

'It was a cold house. Mr Longden had more time to spare. He spent a lot of it listening to music.'

'Mrs Longden, too?'

'She didn't think much of the music.'

'She told you so?'

'Not in words. Sometimes she'd seem to catch my eye.'

'Did you ever have a private conversation with her?'

'Only once. Mr Longden was upstairs, doing some enlarging in his darkroom. I was checking someone's receipts against their day-book. Mrs Longden came into the room to bring me bread and cheese and beer. She led off about how much she hated the house. I was quite taken aback.'

'Did she lead off about her husband, too?'

A dark flush came to his cheeks.

'No. Nothing like that. But I was surprised. She had always been such an uncomplaining sort.'

'Like yourself.'

'I like to oblige people. I like to have plenty to do.'

'It seems to me that Raven and Longden between them have managed that for you. How often in your moonlighting for Matthew Longden did you come across shady book-keeping?'

It was a question that Ernest Weatherhead did not like. Perhaps his answer was a little too emphatic.

'Never, Mr Mosley.'

'What, never? Or hardly ever?'

'Mr Mosley, I only ever saw bits and pieces of anyone's books. Only Mr Longden saw the whole picture.'

'But didn't you sometimes know that he had spotted something in the whole picture? Didn't he ever remark that someone was sailing close to the wind?'

'He would never have said such a thing, Mr Mosley. Mr Longden never said anything that was not proper.'

And suddenly, for no reason that Weatherhead could see, Mosley took the pressure off.

'I suppose not. No. No – that would take a lot of imagining.'

'Mr Mosley – I have a terrible amount of work to do. We have a Sale coming up. I ought to be going round stock.'

Yet Mosley went on talking, went on repeating disconnected questions that he had asked before, not forcefully now, but casually, almost sleepily, as if he had nothing else to do with his afternoon except keep Weatherhead from the routines he was anxious to get at.

It was getting on for four o'clock before Mosley got up and left the shop.

'I tell you, he's overboard this time,' Marsters reported. 'Blown his fuses, gone pancakes, bananas. I don't know what he thinks he's getting out of that Weatherhead. He can't even umpire a cricket match properly now. Bradburn Second are thinking of dropping him.'

'Easier for them than for us,' the ACC said.

'I've had to carpet him for suppressing evidence,' Tom Grimshaw added. 'You'd have thought in the pages of screed he submitted, there'd have been some mention of history repeating itself. Oh, I know that it didn't matter. It was only that German woman, trying to dig her knife into Longden's ribs. But it won't do, will it? One wonders how much else Mosley is keeping to himself.'

Weatherhead had to work late. He had sat listening to Mosley's drowsy voice while the work of the day piled up all round him. At half past four in the afternoon he had only just begun to check a delivery that had been made at ten that morning. At half past five he had not made out a single one of the day's orders. But at least he was able to shoot the bolts of the main door at half past five and shut out the public. He rang Margaret to ask her to keep something warm in the oven for him.

As he walked home the town was closed down and nearly deserted, the sodium lighting imprinting a peculiar lifelessness on the shop-fronts. In an arcade three youths were playing football with a Pepsi-Cola tin. He took a short cut across the park. There was something about the dusty aisles, the litter under the shrubs, that seemed to sap him of spirit.

When he reached home, he saw that there was a light on in the front room. That was unusual at this time of day and on this day of the week. It was not that the Weatherheads were mean about fuel, or that they clung mindlessly to the habits of the lower working class in which they had both been brought up. But it did seem to them that it made sense to economize on the heating of rooms that they did not really need to use.

He was about to put his key in the latch when Margaret opened the door for him. Imperceptibly, she had given up making that sort of gesture years ago. But he soon learned the reason for it: she had to come and forewarn him. Mosley was waiting for him.

101

13

They were trying desperately to get a new legend going in the Plough.

'It's funny they should be talking of bringing a dragon up Kestrel Clough. The old folk were never too keen on that footpath after dark. They reckon Isaac Oldham's grandfather left this pub one night with his hair as black as a crow, and it was white as the driven snow by the time he got home.'

'But that was no dragon he saw. That was Walter Haig's missus, waiting for Walt with a lantern and her copper-stick.'

'Aye, and Jess Oldham fell arse over tip into Walter's lime-bunker. That was why his hair went white.'

Tom Appleyard and Brad Oldroyd were working hard on the dragon. But no legend was ready to emerge yet. It was too soon to anticipate events.

There was, however, a story that had gained general acceptance without any effort on anyone's part. It was assumed that Lottie Pearson had formed one of her broad-minded friendships with someone at the managerial top of the television team. It was generally believed that wherever they had gone, she would be hanging about as a camp-follower. And every man in the Plough was convinced that when the crew came back with their dragon, Lottie Pearson would also be with them.

No one knew who had started this new belief.

Mosley was sitting in one of the Weatherheads' armchairs with his raincoat actually off. The evening was not all that chilly, but Margaret Weatherhead had insisted on switching on one of the bars of their coal-simulating fire at nine o'clock. She could not understand what was making Ernest so late: it was not as if it were the end of year stock-taking. She made very obvious attempts to coax Mosley into giving her some hint as to what it was all about, but she knew very well that if Mosley did not want to be shifted, there would be no shifting him. As far as Margaret Weatherhead was concerned, Mosley was incalculable. Then suddenly, changing his mind for no reason that she could see, he said that he saw no objection to telling her. He did tell her. By the time he had finished, she was twisting her hands together like a neurotic adolescent.

'I can't believe it, Mr Mosley. I just can't believe it of Ernest.'

'I think you'll find he'll tell us about it himself.'

'But what will happen to him, Mr Mosley – what will they do to him?'

'I just can't say, my dear. It's not a situation I've ever come up against before. And the handling of it won't be in my hands.'

'But if he tells you the truth – if he makes a clean breast of it – you'll be able to help him?'

'I can promise you nothing like that. I don't even know myself,' Mosley said. 'And I have a strong feeling that no one's going to take much notice of me. Mind you, it's always good policy to tell the truth. It's always appreciated when they see that you're genuinely trying to help the court.'

'It will have to go to court, will it?'

'Oh, undoubtedly,' Mosley said mournfully.

Which was how she came to be waiting for her husband in a state of distress that she did not look as if she could tolerate much longer.

'Ernest, Mr Mosley is waiting for you. Tell him everything you know, Ernest. Tell him the truth. Everything you know and everything you did. He's told me what it's all about.'

Mosley had sprung to his feet to greet Weatherhead as if they had promised to go out for a drink together.

'What's this all about, Mr Mosley?'

'I must ask you to leave us alone together,' Mosley said to Weatherhead's wife.

She was loth to do that, and it looked for a second or two as if she were going to be difficult. But there was determination in Mosley's eyes, and she was afraid of making things even more difficult for Ernest. She left the room, pulled the door to, stood outside it for an instant, then they heard her go into her kitchen. Weatherhead was now angry, a form of defence that Mosley had never seen him use before.

'What are you playing at today, Mr Mosley? You've been messing me about since this morning. What's this all about?'

'Well, it's about making you late for your supper, for one thing, and I'm sorry about that. But really, the whole thing's in your hands. The sooner you've answered a few little questions, the sooner you'll be settling down with your knife and fork.'

'What questions? You've been asking me questions all day.'

'I think you know, Ernest, that Mrs Pearson has left Matthew Longden.'

'And Queen Anne's dead.'

'There are some curious features. That's why I tried to find out from you the names of anyone that Longden was blackmailing. Besides yourself, that is.'

'He was not blackmailing me.'

'Call it by a kinder name, if it makes it easier to face. It doesn't make the offence any kinder. Lottie Pearson's airline ticket to Amsterdam was found in a Greater Manchester phone-booth.'

'I don't see how that concerns me.'

'It doesn't. It concerns Lottie Pearson. She'd arranged it to happen, to draw our attention to an item of past history – just in case we'd missed it for ourselves. The same thing happened to Betty Longden – only Betty Longden hadn't planted it herself – had she, Ernest?'

Weatherhead was rubbing his thighs with tense hands, but stopped as soon as he realized that he was doing it. 'No comment,' he said.

'It was you who went into that police station and said that you had found her ticket – which Matthew Longden had given you. I can't for a moment imagine that you enjoyed doing it. Early closing day in Bradburn, was it? It must have been one of the most wretched afternoons you've ever spent. I can just see you walking up to that police counter. The very floor-boards must have been lurching under you.'

'No comment.'

'And all because Longden was still threatening to expose you to Roderick Raven. He certainly got his interest on that two-fifty, didn't he – not only by using you for evening after evening as an unpaid audit clerk.'

'I demand to have my solicitor present,' Weatherhead said, which was a ludicrous imitation from dramatic fiction, because the only solicitor he had had to do with was for the conveyancing when he had bought this house.

'You'll set him a pretty problem, Ernest. Accessory after murder is not a charge that's often been handled in Bradburn.'

'I know nothing about any murder.'

'Maybe not. Right hand, left hand. I don't suppose anyone told you where Jack Pearson buried Betty Longden.'

'No comment.'

'*No comment*, Ernest, is one of the prettiest confessions in the annals.'

But Ernest Weatherhead showed a strength of character that Mosley could not break. It was after midnight, and there were only a few token sodium lights left shining as he walked back across the town. A squashed Pepsi-Cola tin lay abandoned in a gutter.

The Weatherheads were still up talking. One of the things that added to their bewilderment was why Mosley had not taken Ernest into custody.

14

Grimshaw had taken Mosley severely to task over the omissions in his reports. It was an offence that was impressed upon the greenest recruits to the force. Even an alteration in a notebook was suspect and could lead to disciplinary action. As it happened, the items concerned were of minor importance, and Grimshaw understood that Mosley's sole intent had been to simplify. But in an officer of Mosley's experience that was a kind of editing that was quite inexcusable. Mosley must watch it in future.

So Mosley was up late after leaving the Weatherheads' home, composing an account for Superintendent Grimshaw in which he explained in a finely chopped logical sequence why he firmly recommended that no immediate action be taken against Weatherhead: to act prematurely would be to forewarn Matthew Longden – and perhaps other principals.

When he had completed this document, it seemed as if Mosley's muse had been over-stimulated by the effort, for he went on composing in his rolling, antithetical English prose. A letter was long overdue to his cousin Samuel, a flourishing police figure, well known amid the wickedness of Hong Kong.

Mosley did not go into his HQ next day. He posted his letters on his way out to the wild country at the head of Hadley Dale. Grimshaw received his by the afternoon delivery. He drew it from its envelope and read it with satisfaction. It was a long, racy and rambling account of minor incidents on the Lancashire–Yorkshire border which he really did not need to know in such detail.

'Sometimes,' he told the ACC, 'I have the distinct impression that Mosley is trying to tell me something. Whatever it is this time, they are going to know about it in the Far East long before we do. What I have here is a newsy updating of his Cousin Sam. It is mainly about dark happenings behind the scenes at the Agricultural Show.'

Mosley went for a country walk up one of the higher reaches of Hadley Dale, over one of the crests down towards the valley bottom beyond. He had to begin his expedition by crossing a corner of Matthew Longden's territory, but he knew the lie of the land intimately enough to achieve it without bringing himself into view from any of Longden's windows. He made a broad detour round the rear of the house, crossed a corner of plantation and began a slow descent by a footpath that had rarely been trodden in the last few years. His way was presently barred by a gate firmly secured by a padlock and several windings of rusted chain.

Mosley climbed this gate – an unathletic and inelegant performance, rolling over the top of it rather than straddling it.

Beyond it, the footpath was even harder to make out than it had been higher up. Thick tangles of brambles straggled out from either bank, tearing savagely at his raincoat. He thrust his hands deep into his pockets and bulldozed his way through a bed of nettles. Further down he squelched through a bog where a hillside spring welled out over the path. After a while he came to an intersection of field paths where two tracks led away from each other to serve the rough grazing of Bottom Farm. Here he had to pass an erosion on the flank of the hill where the rock-face had been washed smooth and concave by centuries of weather. It was not exactly a cave. Limestone caves usually begin as a fault in the rock which admits the destructive water. In this case, the fault had fallen in completely before the water had achieved much. Kestrel's Hole was the beginning of a cave that had collapsed at an early stage of its formation. A skilful man with a camera here could produce a background reminiscent of the world when it was very young indeed. Mosley spent a little time looking round this spot. He kicked about in the undergrowth. He flattened nettles with the side of his foot and inspected the moss that covered the scree beneath them. He tested the weight and equilibrium of a large fallen boulder: it would not rock in its bed. He pushed up his hat, tilting it back from his forehead and stood for a few seconds looking back up the hill.

Then he continued downwards. The ground below him was now merging into the relatively flat bottom of the dale, providing one of the principal pastures of the farm. He heard the steady and arhythmical sounds of a man working with heavy implements against wood and stone. He made his way towards this activity.

'Nah, Isaac.'

'Nah, Jack.'

Isaac Oldham farmed the Bottom, which had once been the home farm of Hadley House. It had been detached from the property when Longden had bought it. Isaac Oldham was known to be wallowing in mortgages and second mortgages. At the moment he was engaged in basic repairs to an unrailed bridge that crossed a ten-foot-wide rivulet.

'You have to be able to turn your hands to anything,

107

nowadays, Isaac.'

'Oh, aye, what with the cost of labour. I can't afford a builder's insurance stamps, let alone his time.'

'You've been at this long, then?'

'A week or two. If I can't get a tractor and trailer across the beck, I'm in trouble next winter.'

Mosley inspected the workmanship with the eye of an apparent expert.

'You saved yourself an overdraft here, Isaac.'

'Aye – and what with my TV earnings –'

'Making you a star next time, are they, then?'

'Nay.'

Isaac laughed – as old friends do laugh together.

'I don't know what they'd use my face and yours for, Jack, save to tan leather for ladies' bags.'

He spat into the stream. 'No. That producer. Forget his name. Round the week before last. Nice enough chap, when he wants to do business with you on his own terms. He wanted to know if I'd an empty sty he could keep a dragon in for a couple of nights. They're going to photograph a sword-fight by moonlight up in the 'Ole. Advertising razor-blades, finest tempered steel. Going to be a real dragon, he reckoned. A big lizard that some bugger has brought back from an expedition. A monitor, did he call it? They're going to do some double-shuffle with their cameras, so it can look like it's breathing fire.'

Oldham stooped to pick up his sledge, groaned, and held his hand to the small of his back.

'I don't mind telling you, Jack, I'm good for anything, these days. He offered me two or three months of my sort of income, just to stable his lizard, and for use of the 'Ole. No wonder razor-blades cost what they do. It'll help to pay for my Saxon gatepost.'

Somewhere on the hillside above them, a curlew called. High in the sky a lark was exalting in a frenzy.

'So how did he come to find the Hole?' Mosley asked him. 'It's not the sort of spot one would just happen on.'

'*She* showed him,' Isaac Oldham said. 'Walked him down there. Between takes, I think they called it. Just the spot for St George to go to work in.'

'Had she often been down that way herself, then?'

'When she first moved into the House, she often came walking, sometimes with Longden, sometimes alone. I used to think to myself, what a good thing they were for each other. Oh, I mean, I know people talk. She had what you might call a reputation. And I felt the same as the rest when she first moved in with him. I thought to myself, he's no different from anyone else, when a breath of air gets in at his crotch. But then I thought, they've both found what they wanted, something that neither of them had had before. And so it went for a few months. She was a gradely woman, when she wanted to be, and when things were going right with her. And there's a lot to be said for Mr Longden, when he's letting himself be a natural man. But then he had to screw down into himself again, I don't know why: pretending he's something he isn't, when all he's got to do is be what he *is*.'

Oldham would not have had it that he was philosophizing. He had never ranked as a happy man, yet he seemed sure of his recipes for other men's happiness. A hare came rushing in a diagonal line over the far distance of one of his fields. A dog, someone's stray from the village, was hurtling madly after it, a hopeless chase, its prey gaining a yard in every ten. Mosley and Oldham stopped talking to watch, unexcited, uninvolved.

'Of course, what I've always said about Lottie –' Oldham said. He used her Christian name as if she were a remote but not unloved member of his own family '– she made a wrong step once in her life. That soldier she wed was no use to her. And it was a wrong step for all time. In her own country, among her own kind, she'd happen have had a different look about her. But I understand why she never went back. It would be like me coming back home, if I'd done something daft.'

'And what can you tell me about the going of her?' Mosley asked.

'Nowt. She didn't come down this way. My dogs would have told me. But then, she'd no call to come this way, had she? I do know that a week or two before he went, before we'd heard owt about spacemen, she was down here walking on her own. And she was poking round the Hole quite a bit. I thought to myself, aye, she's wondering –'

'We've all been wondering for years,' Mosley said. 'And the night Betty Longden was last seen in the Dale: what did your dogs tell you about that, Isaac?'

'To stay indoors and mind my own business, Jack.'

Tom Appleyard and Brad Oldroyd were the story-tellers of the Dale, and in their way its historiographers. There were few tales about mind-stretching events since the end of the war that one or both of them had not had a hand in, inventing – and improving. Some of the best of their tales had blossomed when they were together; and yet Brad's approach to the art was quite different from Tom's. Brad Oldroyd could spin his ideas out of frosty air; Tom Appleyard needed something to trigger his off. He had to see a sheep and a mushroom to think of putting one beneath the other. But Brad Oldroyd did not need to see an empty cemetery to start counting the ghosts in it. Mosley went to see Oldroyd first.

Brad was one of those weather-seasoned men who eat heartily all their lives without putting on an ounce of unneeded fat. He had looked sixty since he was forty, and would go on looking sixty if he lived to be eighty-five. He was a master carpenter, and could have earned good money at his trade, but he preferred odd-jobbing because he needed variety. He liked to have a different set of tools in his hand from week to week, he always said, and when Mosley found him, he was putting the finishing touches to some new guttering on Walter Passmore's gable-end.

Nah, Brad – Nah, Jack – Atta weel? – There's folk's wuss –

Mosley could drop easily into the vernacular of men the likes of whom he had been to school with.

'What do you remember, Brad, about Betty Longden, before she went?'

'I remember when she came. We didn't take to her at first – but that was only from the manner of her speech.'

Oldroyd lit a three-quarter-inch dog-end that he took from an old Elastoplast tin.

'Longden speaks the same English as the Queen, but you can tell he's spent all his life in these parts. But she was Down South to the marrow. Yet she wanted to know folk. You could tell that she wanted to talk: not like Longden. When he gave you the time of day, you could tell it was because he thought he ought to.'

He flicked a fallen leaf off his boot.

'I mind after the Vegetable Show, she was helping dry up in the kitchen tent with my missus and one or two others. But he came and called her out of it. She wasn't supposed to muck in. He played old Harry with her on their way to his car.'

'There was supposed to be a man in the case,' Mosley said. 'In a cafe in Bradcaster. Did he ever show his nose in Hadley Dale to your knowledge?'

'Somebody would have said.'

'*Was* there a man, Brad?'

'You know me, Jack. I've told so many yarns in my time, I'm not all that good when it comes to straight talking. There's nothing like a good tale – bar a better one. Not that I ever made anything up about the Longdens, you understand. But if you ask me what I believed, I'd say no: there was never a man.'

'So give me the benefit of a bit of your story-telling now, Brad. How could someone be seen going to Amsterdam, and yet not go to Amsterdam?'

Oldroyd gave it some thought.

'You'd need an out-of-work actress,' he said. 'She wouldn't need to know *why* she was doing it, would she? If she had any sense, she wouldn't ask.'

Walter Passmore looked out of his window at the pair of them. He was the sort of man to reflect that he was not paying Brad to stand talking.

'When did the milk of love start going off between Longden and Lottie, Brad?'

Brad picked up his hammer and a masonry nail, but did not turn back yet to his guttering. 'Who's to tell? She was too natural for him, that was my view. All right; she taught him to be natural in his bedroom, which did him no harm. And while that was a novelty with him, he had to keep her sweet to keep the pot boiling. But she said things in a funny way in public, wasn't going to snub her old pals in the village just because he said so. Vulgar – that's what Longden thought of being natural.

It couldn't have lasted, Jack – and it didn't. I'd better be getting up this ladder, before Passmore stops me a quarter.'

Tom Appleyard had been a time-keeper at the quarry, and in his retirement he read a lot, biographies mostly: Lloyd George, the desert generals, Toscanini. When Mosley called, he was watching a schools broadcast: 'Music Workshop'.

The talk did not follow the same lines as with Brad; but it arrived at the same landmarks.

'*Was* there a man, Tom?'

'Certainly there was a man.'

'You speak as if you know.'

'I do know. I saw him.'

'Here in the Dale?'

'No, no. He never came here. I'm as sure of that as I am of this chair I'm sitting on. If he'd come up here, there'd have been all hell on up at the House, and the Plough would have been full of it.'

'Did they have rows up at the House? Did anybody ever hear them?'

'My daughter used to go up to give a hand sometimes – when they were spring-cleaning and the like. There was always an atmosphere.'

Appleyard took a plug of black twist from a jar on his mantelpiece and began shredding it on to a sheet of paper on a corner of his table.

'Not so much rowing as not rowing, if that doesn't sound too daft. Tight lips. Backs turned. The row had gone on behind the scenes, maybe yesterday, maybe last week, wasn't forgiven yet. Maybe never would be forgiven.'

'What about, do you know? What sort of thing?'

'Do rows like that have to be about anything? She didn't like living in Hadley Dale. He'd promised her paradise here. Things were going to be different, once they'd moved. But nothing had changed.'

'What did she want changed?'

'He went on with the things that he wanted to do. What she wanted to do was always out of the question. She wanted women from the village up at the House for a play-reading group. He wouldn't have it.'

'And this man?'

'I saw him in Bradcaster. Once. I'd taken the deeds to the bank for safe keeping, after I'd paid off this mortgage. They were upstairs in the cafe. Enjoying each other's company. That was all that could be said of it. I'd never seen her so relaxed. She was quite unaware anyone was watching her.'

'When was this, Tom?'

'Six or seven months before she went.'

'You saw them once. That doesn't make it regular, does it?'

'No, but it was. That tale got round. Not *my* telling.'

'So who else was there, Tom?'

'There were three women from the Dale at one of the tables. They'd been at some women's get-together. Need I say more?'

'Can you describe this man?'

But that was not very successful. A gentleman, Appleyard would say. Tailored suit, of a good cut, but not showy. Could have been a year or two younger than Betty Longden. Looked as if he might be a professional man. There were no details that would help pick him up all these years later – if one knew where to begin.

'And what about her manner of going from Hadley Dale, Tom?'

'She can't have been driven away from the House, else we'd all have known all about it. She could have walked out of the village, been picked up in a car.'

'What about her bags?'

'I hadn't given that much thought. There could have been ways and means, I suppose. There are men about who would have helped her out for a quiet quid or two. Ted Hunter was working for them at the time. He might have lent her a hand. But I shouldn't say that. I don't know.'

'And then what happened?'

'Well, there was news of her in Manchester, I always understood. Then didn't she fly to Amsterdam? Then they got lost from there. I'd think there'd be a few dozen ways a couple could do that. Didn't Matthew Longden hire a private detective to try to pick up their trail? Throwing his money away? You seem to be taking a lot of interest in Betty Longden this morning, Jack –'

'It's Lottie Pearson, Tom. She's been making it all happen again. She must have picked up this, that and the other idea in her years at the House. Maybe it all suddenly clicked into place. I can't make my mind up whether it's us she's trying to tell – or whether she's trying to drive Matthew out of his mind. But before very long, I reckon she's going to chuck another link in the chain at us. And I want to be ready when that happens.'

Crime was rarely rife in Mosley's area. It came in patches. At a time when he did not want that to happen, he was called away from Hadley Dale to attend to a rash of housebreaking, down in Hayburn Market. He always disliked it when individuals of fixed local habits went walkabout, started showing an interest in places where they did not belong. There had been strangers in Hayburn Market. The tally of property stolen may not have suggested an affluent community – or a tasteful one – but it included articles cherished by their owners: Albert Pickford's life-tally of bowls medals, for one item, and a carriage clock that had belonged to Alice Tweed's godmother.

Mosley listened at patient length to the unhappiness of those who had been deprived. He listened to other men's talk in the bus-station snack bar, to whispers in the public reading-room. He heard who had been in Hayburn Market without convincing business.

Bertie Lee, from Strubshaw Bottoms. Alf Carter from Gunley. Mosley remembered seeing them in Crawdon, the night Joe Ormerod had driven him home after they had dug up Lottie Pearson's oddments. He had been dead tired. He had done nothing about it. But he had not failed to take note that Jack Pearson made up the trio.

Mosley took a bus to Strubshaw Bottoms, then another to Gunley. The interviews followed familiar lines. Lee and Carter were in possession of much of the property concerned, but they indignantly denied any knowledge of it. It then became a routine process to jolly villains along from one admission to the lot. That was something in which Mosley had always excelled, and in this case he had an additional lever. Jack Pearson had not been with them in the Hayburn Market theatre of operations, but he had been their companion in other activities. Therefore Mosley could casually let it slip that he knew about Pearson – which to Bertie Lee and Alf Carter looked like some kind of magic. They assumed that Mosley, knowing this, also knew a lot more. They gave up the fight.

The next stage was to persuade them how advantageous it would be for them to ask for other cases to be taken into consideration. It would not wipe the slate clean, but it would temper justice with mercy – and please those at headquarters who liked neat records of property retrieved.

And it was at this juncture that the exercise took an interesting turn. The laborious statements of Bertie and Alf showed that they, together with Pearson, had been active on two nights a week throughout the summer months. But very little of their work had been done on Mosley's territory. Most of it had been perpetrated in regions protected by Chief Inspector Marsters. They had been consistently defeating Marsters since shortly after Easter. Mosley left a copy of his report, suitably marked *For Information*, on Chief Inspector Marsters's desk.

Then he went to the remand wing at Bradcaster to see Pearson again. This time it was not about robberies that he wanted to talk to him.

Hunter's case came up before the Bradburn justices, Colonel Mortimer presiding. Colonel Mortimer told Hunter how narrowly he had escaped going to prison. He would be fined £250. But despite the fact that men of substance and integrity had been prepared to speak up in his favour, the Bench did not feel, in view of the callousness of the attack on young Bernard, that it would be safe to return the boy to his parents at present. He would therefore be committed to the Care of the Authority. It was open to the Hunters, if they wished, to appeal to the Crown Court against this Order. Hunter appeared to be living up admirably to his promises of law-abiding sobriety. If this proved not to be a flash in the pan, Colonel Mortimer felt confident that perhaps, in six months or a year . . .

Mosley took note of Hunter's eyes as he left the court. They did not promise well for the Queen's Peace.

15

Mosley happened to be loitering idly in the town centre of Bradburn late one afternoon when a small convoy drew up. There were three private cars, one Dormobile, one horse-box and a van painted with the exotic lettering of a contemporary publicity company.

The head man of the concern was of middle age and had a thick thatch of black hair. He was wearing a tee-shirt that suggested a connection with the Free University of Stoke Newington and he was driving in canvas beach-shoes whose laces were frayed down to their last viable strand. Mosley had discovered from a Directory of Company Directors that the man's name was Teagle.

'If I might just have a word with you, sir.'

Teagle mistook him for a town idler and showed no inclination to be forthcoming.

'I am a police officer.'

Mosley made a motion to get out his warrant card. Teagle waved it aside.

'It's all right to park here for a minute or two, surely?'

'It isn't a question of parking,' Mosley said.

'I hope you're not intending to waste my time, officer. I've a lot on my plate at this moment.'

Mosley muttered something that Teagle did not quite catch. He was not meant to. Mosley's approach always gave him a working advantage over men who could not decide how to make head or tail of him.

'Look – I'm carrying a very special animal in that horse-box. I need to get it to its quarters as soon as I can.'

'Yes, sir. That comes under the Cinematographic Films (Animals) Act, 1937, Section One. I have arranged for our friends from the RSPCA to come and look over your arrangements.'

A job for uniform branch; but Mosley had always taken a flexible view of such protocol. There was such a thing as finding one's way into a case, and he had a very thorough knowledge of odd by-ways of the law.

'If that's all it is,' Teagle said, 'go ahead. In my own interests I've taken all available advice. You don't think I'd take risks with a valuable animal like this, do you? You wouldn't think so, if you knew what I'd paid for insurance.'

'That's not all it is,' Mosley said.

'Well – do you mind if I pop down for a pee? I'm breaking my neck for one.'

Mosley waited meekly at the top of the urinal steps.

'Now, sir, I would prefer you to accompany me to the Bradburn police station.' And he muttered something else that was not properly audible.

'If you insist. But I shall stand on my rights. I would regard it as illegal detention to be taken to Bradburn police station, or anywhere else, without being shown good cause. Have you a warrant? Do you propose charging me with an offence?'

'I shall be charging you, sir.'

'With what?'

'Look, sir, I don't think we ought to talk here. We are beginning to attract a crowd.'

Not more than eight people, five of them children, were now standing watching. Other members of Teagle's team had got out of their vehicles and were making for the public lavatories. Mosley appeared to ignore them; he did however take note that Lottie Pearson did not seem to be one of the passengers.

Mosley conducted Teagle across Bradburn on foot. The Bradburn police headquarters was not one of those airy showpieces with thermoplastic floor-tiles and pot plants in slatted holders. It was a bizarrely overcrowded Victorian hulk and had once been adequate for an inspector, a sergeant, and the very few constables who were not out getting wet and cold on the streets. Mosley poked his head into one dusty room after another before finding a kind of enlarged cupboard in which they could talk.

'I am anxious to help you, Inspector. I have nothing to gain by breaking the law, or by being suspected of so doing. I will give you an honest answer to anything you want to know.'

There was, it seemed, no qualification to his desire to co-operate, yet there was a certain nerviness about Teagle. It might have been the brittleness of a man who had something on his mind, and who hoped that this policeman was not working round to the same subject.

Mosley lowered his head in what might have been a kind of humility. Or it could have been congenital imbecility.

'Mrs Pearson?' he asked.

'Mrs Pearson?'

The name appeared to mean nothing to Teagle. But then he remembered.

'Oh, you mean Lottie?' He smiled, as if at some whimsical reminiscence.

'Have you brought her with you?'

'Brought her with me? Inspector – why on earth should I have brought her with me?'

'I'd like to know what contact you've had with her since you left your last location; or, indeed, since you left this location.'

'What contact do you expect me to have had, for God's sake? Inspector – what do you think I am? And what is the purpose of this interview?'

Mosley simply sat looking at him.

'Inspector – I have halted in Bradburn so that my colleagues can answer calls of nature. Also, in case there were laggards, so that we could stay close together along the difficult road up to Hadley Dale. We have a unique animal aboard, and I want to get it settled into its quarters. Now – if we could dispose of what business you have with me –'

'Just as soon as a charge-room is vacant.'

'Perhaps you would give me some inkling of the charges.'

'I shall be formally cautioning you that you are not compelled to make any statement – though there are numerous witnesses who will leave you little room for manoeuvre. I understand that you are the owner of a dog that chased grazing sheep on a date of which I will remind you as soon as I can put my hand on the papers. And while we are about it, you may also care to let me have the names of those of your associates who were involved in breaking down fencing with a length of co-axial cable. Also with failing to stop and report damage to a gatepost of historical significance.'

16

A highlight of the Bradburn summer season is the cricket match that is played annually between the elected members of the Borough Council and an eleven selected from among the municipal employees. It is a throwback to a more paternalistic and patronizing age. The Councillors play in top hats and long black frock-coats, strongly redolent of the camphor in which they are stored for this single yearly airing. The rude mechanicals from the corporation yards can always count on a salting of skill and strength, so it is considered a fair handicap for them to take the field in female costume. And there are subtle strategists in the Treasurer's and Surveyor's offices who can bring strains of extempore caprice to the field. For many years the employees used to appear as elderly spinsters, hampered by voluminous skirts and long strings of beads that became entangled with the handles of their bats. Since the permissive sixties they have tended to walk out on the green looking as if they are about to ask the umpires if they would care for a good time. The sight of the Town Hall doorkeeper, with a glimpse of apishly hairy leg between the tops of his pipe-clayed pads and the hem of his mini-skirt has had wolf-whistles shaking the decorum of the pavilion enclosure. It stands to sense that Mosley is always asked to preside at one of the wickets. But a

119

regrettable interruption to this year's match caused him to default at the judgement end for the second time this season.

The Mayoress had bowled the ceremonial opening ball. The batsman had had to walk six yards out of his crease to tap it for an impudent single. His Worship the Mayor had been stumped twice, but Mosley had given him loudly and provocatively *Not Out*, it being an honoured convention that the wearing of the chain gave him three lives. The wicket-keeper was wearing an Afro-style wig and his false bosom had shifted like ballast in the hold of a distressed steamer.

It was at this moment that the peace of the afternoon was dissipated by the arrival on the ground of a motor-cycle whose exhaust reminded spectators of a Boeing 747 about to raise 600 passengers and their baggage from the ground. Two minutes later, the rider, obviously no respecter of the national game, was striding out to the wicket as the bowler was actually starting to run. He was encased in a massive helmet and plastic clothing of avant-garde fashion that made it look as if another Martian sortie had been mounted. Square leg was heard to inform him that Venus was second on the left.

The invader made his direct way to Mosley, to whom he said something that was inaudible through his visor. Mosley gesticulated fiercely, but without immediate effect. It was only when the Mayor threatened the aeronaut comically with his bat that the thought came to him of unbuckling his helmet. A number of players crowded forward to produce a confusion of help. The visitor was now seen to be PC Ormerod, his beetling brows offering violence all round.

'You'd better come,' he said to Mosley. 'He's gone berserk.'

'Who has?'

'He has.'

'Who's he?'

'Hunter. He's locked himself and his wife in their cottage. He's got a shot-gun, and he says he's got dynamite from the quarry. He's going to blow them up at six o'clock if his kid hasn't been delivered to his front door by that time.'

'Have you reported this to division?'

'They're going to send as many men as they can spare from the Foxlow Steam Rally.'

'I doubt the wisdom of that. In this mood, Hunter would make mince-meat of them.'

'Sergeant Beaver was on the desk when I rang through. He says the best thing would be for you to come up to Hadley Dale and talk to Hunter. He says he might listen to you.'

Mosley nodded, as if it were usual for an inspector to take orders from a desk-sergeant. He spoke to the two captains and the other umpire and three minutes later was on the pillion of Ormerod's machine, his short little arms grimly holding on to the slippery plastic of Joe's futuristic coat.

It was a ride that deserved the accompaniment of a Wagnerian tone-poem. A hurricane beat into Mosley's face and filled the flapping legs of his trousers. They took corners with a centripetal verve, at an angle from which it seemed they would never right themselves. They overtook articulated lorries with inches to spare. Round one of the zigzag corners of Crawdon they mounted a pavement to negotiate a milk-float. They performed a classical broadside on the sandy shoulder of the Stonemill Bend.

But Joe delivered Mosley eventually within the central open space of Hadley Dale village. A panda car was discreetly parked in the lee of the post office. A uniformed town inspector called Spears had been sent out to take charge, and set about evacuating every house within a fifty-yards radius of the Hunters' cottage, and despatching the residents under cover. But except for one deaf old man, and an elderly woman who refused to budge, every such house was already vacant. The word had gone round, and Hadley Dale bore a resemblance to a melancholy ghost village.

Spears was an officious officer who never liked to be far from a telephone that connected him with orders from above. He recognized Mosley when he came out from behind the shelter of Ormerod's shoulder-blades.

'There may be nothing for you to do after all. The squire has gone in there.'

'Squire?'

'The chap from the big house. What's his name? Longden. He seemed to know what he's about. He's been in there a good half-hour now, and all's quiet. Now that you're here, I think I'll just put my nose in that pub round the corner. That's perhaps where everybody is. They may be taking advantage. Some of these people seem to think that licensing hours don't apply in country districts.'

Longden, it seemed, had come down to the village for some essential from the shop, of which his stocks had run low. On learning what Hunter was up to, he had announced that he was going in to reason with him. Tom Appleyard, who was waiting his turn at the counter, had tried to tell him what was certain to happen: that Hunter, in his present mood, was likely to be even further inflamed by the sight of one of the ruling classes.

'All that Hunter needs is the sight of calm authority,' Longden said.

No one in the shop chose to argue with him. They all wanted to get their supplies and be away. Taking a second's rest each time he put his stick to the ground, Longden walked openly and slowly across the space in front of the Hunters' windows. It was like the climax of *High Noon*. The barrels of Hunter's shot-gun appeared under the flap of his letter-box. He fired, and shot licked the dust wide of Longden. Longden ignored the gesture in finest cavalier fashion. He opened Hunter's gate, his crippled steps adding dignity to his style as he walked up the stone path. The shot-gun waved from side to side with the impatience of an irritable man. Longden gripped the muzzle and thrust it superciliously in out of sight. There was some delay in opening the door. But he was let in – and immediately became an additional hostage.

Inspector Spears came back from the Plough in his brown leather gloves, carrying his leather-covered swagger-cane.

'There's only the landlord there. It seems that all the rest have gone to some place that they call Kestrel Clough. It appears that there's some sort of filming going on there. Seems to me the cameras would find more action here.'

For all the signs of life that rose from it now, the Hunters' cottage might have been uninhabited. The merest wisp of white smoke crept up from its chimney-cowl. And that might have been the product of a banked-up fire whose owners were away for the day.

'If we go on doing nothing,' Mosley said, 'he might feel he

has to remind us of his existence: a shot through the ceiling, perhaps another across the square. All Longden has done is to give him extra bargaining power.'

'You know Longden well, do you?'

'We've met.'

'And you don't think Hunter will listen to him?'

'He's most likely to put his back up more than it is already.'

'Let's leave things alone for a while,' Spears said. 'It's still a long time off six o'clock. While Longden is with him, no blood's being shed. They'll be here from the Steam Rally before long. When we see what forces we've got, we can make some sort of plan.'

'We'll send Ormerod to flag them down before they arrive. Hunter had better not see them before they're ready to strike. This may not seem very real at the moment: but I assure you it is.'

Explosion and death might not seem very credible in such a setting: a stone squat village as deserted as if no one had been willing to tear himself away from his television screen. Yet in one of the cottages, a man who had possibly murdered his wife was playing the phlegmatic hero. He was being held at gun-point and with gelignite by a crazed and dangerous bully who had almost certainly known the facts of that murder, if murder it had been. It was a curious situation. And in a field beyond the edge of the village, the curlew, a summer visitor, was calling as if the world were at peace.

'And what would be your solution, left to yourself?' Spears asked.

'I'd go down to Bradburn for the boy. I'd tell Hunter I was going to do that, and plead with him for more time if necessary. Hunter won't hurt the boy – not today; never again, in my book. Under cover of their reunion, our forces would act as opportunity offered: to isolate Hunter.'

'Unthinkable,' Spears said.

Mosley looked at him with dog-like, pitying eyes, more eloquent than verbiage.

'We could not possibly be associated with such a thing. I wouldn't even care to suggest it to HQ – playing with the life of a child who is in official care.'

Mosley looked away. He did not seem disposed to press the plan.

'Listen!'

They heard a distant car-engine. Spears stepped back into a stretch of the street that was not visible from Hunter's windows, to halt the new arrivals. But it might just be someone from Hadley Dale, back from shopping. Or, with luck, it could be elements of the Foxlow contingent. They heard the vehicle's gears deal with the hairpin entry into the village. They followed its progress as far as Well Street, which would bring it round by the western edge of the square. And then it cornered into sight – a J-registration Cortina, with two women in it.

Spears semaphored vigorously for the car to stop, ran in full view across the square when it ignored him. Shot whipped up dust from the road, wide of Spears's feet. The second barrel might perhaps have been aimed at the car, but the only damage was a panel scratched by a ricochet. Crouching behind his front door, peering through a two-inch-square gap, Hunter could take no sort of aim. The car lurched from a startled hand on the steering, then righted itself without decelerating. Spears swung round behind it, shouting uselessly.

There were two women in the front seat. Lottie Pearson was driving. At her side sat a figure who had changed since Mosley had last seen her: grey hair, perhaps, a more colourful, more youthful summer frock than she had been accustomed to wear about Hadley Dale village. But she was still stately by nature and by breeding: Betty Longden.

The car shot away with an impudent bleep of its throttle. Spears turned round, still infuriated, looking at Mosley as if it had all been his fault. Joe Ormerod came up from somewhere.

'What's to stop me from working my way round the hummock, to try to break in at the back?'

'Both barrels,' Mosley said shortly. 'Sometimes when I look at you, Joe, I wonder whether you're mortal. I've no wish to put it to the test this afternoon.'

He turned to Spears.

'You'll have a radio on net in your car? I'd better get in touch with Tom Grimshaw. Maybe it'd be worth asking him about bargaining with young Hunter.'

Spears did not object to this – as long as it was Mosley who was sticking his neck out. Throwing responsibility on to a senior was familiar ground to him. One of Isaac Oldham's cows lowed beyond the horizon. The ducks on the pond did not seem to care how many rolls of high explosive Hunter was harbouring behind his front door. One of Tom Appleyard's pigeons was working hard, but without response, trying to gain the attention of his lady-love.

Mosley stood for a moment and studied the ducks: he always found ducks irresistible. Then he walked without haste towards Spears's panda, his coat swinging behind him to give an illusion of nonchalance. He might have been some rural insurance collector, about to tick off weekly industrial contributions at cottagers' doors.

But no sooner was he inside the car than things started to happen. The starter motor failed twice, then the engine fired. The panda leaped forward, three-point turned, then came back past Spears and Ormerod, driving with wide throttle in bottom gear past Hunter's house. Hunter, firing now from a window, scored his first hit of the afternoon, a double delivery of shot that wrought havoc with the immaculate panels of Spears's rear door, but did no other damage. Spears winced.

Mosley did a right-angled turn that had the Escort lurching as he drove out of Hunter's effective range, while Hunter was still fumbling with his breech. Spears and Ormerod, now alone in the village street, were left to interpret as best they could such sounds as carried in to them on the hot afternoon air.

They may perhaps have deduced that Mosley did not travel more than a few hundred yards out of the village before pulling up again, at the bottom of the hairpins, where he did a U-turn and parked on a verge that danced with campion and cow-parsley.

There was then nothing for them to interpret except an hour and a half's summer silence, until a labouring heavy vehicle began the slow climb from Crawdon. Did the waiting policemen know that it must be the Saturday shoppers' bus returning? Did Joe Ormerod realize that his wife must be on it, accompanied by a selection of their offspring? Joe may even have been salivating at the thought that his weekly sea-food ration was approaching.

But then something happened that apparently imperilled, or at least delayed his treat. The bus stopped at the foot of the hairpin approaches. Was it being hi-jacked by some bandit ravenous for cockles? Or might Mosley be standing out in the road, holding up his hand?

Did Spears – who did not know his Hadley Dale – realize that if someone did not intercept the public service vehicle, the square would in a very few minutes be an untidy sprawl of housewives and children, a sight likely to excite Hunter, or at least dangerously to disturb him? There was no telling what Hunter might do, piqued by the sight of a crowd of normal people, caught at an insouciant moment in their normal lives.

The engine of the bus did not start up again, but the car-engine did. Spears braced his body to a stance of alertness by a corner of wall beyond Hunter's arc of fire. This had now become a sort of tactical HQ, with Joe Ormerod parked close to him, sitting on his motor-cycle, which was up on its back-stand.

Five o'clock passed. From behind the window of the old woman who had refused to leave her home could be heard the announcements of sports results. A pair of Tom Appleyard's doves flew from one flank of the square to the other, and then flew back again. In spite of all Spears's warnings, the old woman now came out of her house and went to knock on a neighbour's door, in full view of Hunter. Spears fulminated, but nothing happened. Getting no reply, the woman went home again. The car could be heard climbing the hairpins. It would soon come in sight. The barrels of Hunter's gun appeared again at the window and steadied themselves. Spears signalled to Ormerod with a wave of his gloves and Joe silently unstraddled his cycle to take up a crouching position between Spears and the forthcoming arena.

The car appeared at the top of the road that led down to the square. It was being driven slowly, and stopped some forty yards away. Spears thought he could see more than one person in it, though at the distance he could not make out who it was that Mosley had with him. After the shortest of halts, the panda began to come on again, very slowly indeed, turning at right angles some twenty yards short of Hunter's. Mosley's silhouette was now clearly identifiable by his hat. The gun barrels were now in full command of Mosley, the car and its passenger.

The car now carried out a curious manoeuvre, first veering to the right, then coming round to the left in the tightest turning-circle of which it was capable. At a snail's pace it pulled up level with a manhole-cover which was almost the spot on which Hunter had his gun trained at the ready. Then the angle of the muzzle changed and there were the sounds of the drawing of bolts. Joe Ormerod, still on his haunches, looked sleepily sideways, as if something of interest might be going to happen soon. The gun changed its axis again, obviously drawing a bead on Mosley's head. Ormerod did not stir.

Mosley opened his door, and his legs issued forth with about the same athletic agility he had shown when climbing the gate in Kestrel Clough. He turned his head to say something to someone inside: a boy, who appeared to be trying to withdraw his body into himself, as if frightened to death. Mosley shut the car door and came out alone, walking slowly until he was half-way between the manhole-cover and the house. There he stopped to take out his pipe and fiddle about in its bowl with the spike of his knife. He fumbled for a box of matches. Shreds of over-packed tobacco fell over his clothing.

'Longden is to come out first. He's to carry your gun – and any other weapon you have in there. I shan't let the lad out until I have those in my hands.'

Hunter did not comply. His gun moved from side to side indecisively. Perhaps a conference was going on in the house. Perhaps Longden was trying to be persuasive: it was possible to imagine that his arguments might be ponderous.

'I want to see the kid first, Mosley.'

Mosley did not exactly nod; he made a sort of bow in the direction of Hunter. He turned on his heel in an elderly person's parody of the parade-ground movement and halted to put another match to his pipe with his back to the house.

Then he walked slowly towards the car. The door of the house opened. Mosley did not turn to see what was happening. Matthew Longden came out carrying the gun, broken open at the breech, in his other a hand a faggot of dynamite sticks, looking like a bundle of fasces. The house door remained ajar.

Hunter had not yet made himself visible.

Mosley had reached the car, began to open the rear door. He leaned in to help the boy out, masking his slender-legged figure.

The cottage door opened and Hunter stood framed in it, in a rough working shirt with his buttons undone. Yet his hair was incongruously brilliantined.

'Send him over!' he shouted.

'Come and fetch him,' Mosley said.

Hunter began to come down the short length of his garden path.

'If you try anything, Mosley!'

Mosley waited, the boy still hidden behind him. Hunter came out on to the pavement, began to cross to the car. And that was when Joe Ormerod sprang. The way Joe was crouching looked awkward. It seemed about the most inept possible position for a man contemplating action. Surely he was cramping himself out of all hope of mobility. But there was more than one respect in which Joe Ormerod did not seem to be made as other men are. He did not seem to need to flex his muscles. They uncoiled like steel springs and hurled him ballistically at Hunter from obliquely behind him. He took Hunter's knees in a rugger tackle, brought the big quarryman down in the dust. Then Ormerod's hand swept and Hunter's face was crushed into the tarmac. Ormerod clouted Hunter behind the ear, following that with an uppercut under the nose. His third blow dislocated Hunter's jaw from behind. By now, Spears was calling Ormerod off, coming up with his handcuffs.

Mrs Hunter, agitated, was now out on her path.

'Hey! That's not my boy!'

It was very obviously not Bernard Hunter. It was that product of the Ormerods' union who resembled his father to the point of burlesque. Mosley had brought him off the shoppers' bus.

'Bernard was not available at such short notice,' Mosley said. 'But I think you'll be getting him back, once his father's arrived where he's going.'

Then he turned to Spears.

'Run me down to Bottom Farm, will you? I have a date with two interesting women.'

17

Spears drove Mosley into Oldham's farmyard – a yard seemingly deserted of all activity save for three or four self-supporting pullets who were scratching for brandling worms on a dunghill. Hunter was in the back seat, manacled, alternatively moaning about the injuries he had received from Ormerod and making wild efforts at self-justification. Spears and Mosley might have little in common, but they snapped at him simultaneously to hold his peace.

'It's Kestrel Hole you want to be watching, Mr Mosley. You'll have a few tons of stone to shift, and you'll find what you'll find. I could tell you a thing or two – and I'm in the clear. Can't we go somewhere where we can talk, Mr Mosley?'

'You've talked before – and what did it amount to?'

'You talk to Betty Longden. She'll tell you. I saved her life.'

'Oh, aye?'

There were a few cars parked about the yard of Bottom Farm and the adjacent fields had been used as a right of way by the sightseers who had flooded in to see the cameras at work. Small groups of these were already beginning to drift back from the scene of the filming, which they had begun to find slow, repetitive and disillusioning.

'It's faked from start to finish,' someone was saying.

'You can't believe a thing you see on the box.'

'If that's a dragon, I don't know what the fuss is about. It looks half asleep to me.'

'And did you see who else was up there?'

'And how about her for a Princess? Fair, fat and past it. Not my idea of Fairyland.'

'I can't see what they're thinking of.'

'And the other one, too –'

'I notice Longden wasn't showing his face.'

Mosley got out of the car, and Spears drove off for Bradburn. One of those who was not going to let his daily round be upset by a troupe of strolling players was Oldham. Mosley could see him, still working on his bridge, some three hundred yards away, and removed from the main axis of traffic. Mosley made his way over to him.

'Nah, Isaac.'

'Nah, Jack.'

'Looks a bit like Easter Monday with these crowds.'

'Aye – and I've seen who's come too. I'd just gone back to my shed for another yard of sand when their car drew up. Who'd have ever thought of seeing those two together? What's it all about, Jack?'

'I don't know yet, Isaac. But it's to do with the Hole.'

'Aye, well – it's a hole that's been there a long time, Jack.'

Mosley stumped across the tussocky grass towards the collapsed cave mouth that men called Kestrel Clough. Teagle had somehow managed to shepherd the sightseers on to an opposite flank, leaving the heap of fallen stone free to serve as his stage. The crowd was remarkably silent, as if what they were observing demanded respect.

A cardboard cut-out, a profile of the dragon, had been propped up against a wooden framework, behind which had been fixed a cylinder of gas and a flame-throwing nozzle. But this was not in use at the moment. The cameras were fixed on a scene which, according to the figures on the clapper-board, was about to be shot for the twenty-eighth time.

Lottie Pearson was bound to a pillar of stone, and Teagle was urging her to register horror as she caught sight of a paint-mark on the rock-face where the dragon was later to be superimposed. It had been a bold stroke, picking Lottie as heroine. She was very far removed indeed from the popular conception of a medieval female lead. Buxom, broad-boned and broad-featured, and not so very long ago past the forty-year watershed, she was undeniably on the sunset side of youth and beauty. In casting her, Teagle had shown a touch of real genius. She was quite candidly sexy, with a hint of drowsy repletion against a well-upholstered shoulder. Teagle had found her a blonde wig that recalled her hair-style of twenty years ago. She was big-bosomed, conveying a sense of matronly luxuriance, of maternal as well as conjugal loving. Was this what she had taught Matthew Longden to enjoy in the prime of their time together? Was this what she had offered Teagle, knowing that all that interested him would be short-term transports – while she won him to her cause?

Mosley thought he could see at last the answer to a question that had been troubling him: why had Teagle been so irrationally insistent on denying that Lottie would be joining his party here? Why had he expressed such unconvincing surprise that Mosley should connect her with him at all? It could only be because Lottie had promised him something that had to be kept from the knowledge of the police until the critical moment. And what could that be but the chance, as a film-making man, to shoot some sequence that would rank as an epoch-shaking scoop?

And it had to be concerned with Kestrel Clough. Only a few minutes ago, Isaac Oldham had been saying that. Jack Pearson, when Mosley had questioned him recently in his remand cell, had pointed in the same direction – after a fashion.

Mosley was uneasy about Pearson. There had been something strange and untypical about him on this occasion. It was rare for Mosley to fail with a criminal as naïve and gullible as Jack. If he had been using his normal methods, Mosley would not in fact have judged it a failure – yet. All that was wanted was more time. Mosley had usually all the time in the world, where all that was needed was time. In the normal run of events, he would have paid another visit to Jack Pearson – and another and another, until such time as Jack had come round to his way of thinking. Had he not taken his time with Ernest Weatherhead?

Jack Pearson had always been so easy in the past: but this time he would not allow himself to be tripped. He was drawing strength and staying power from a pocket of fear such as Mosley had never seen in him before. It was a pocket of fear that was tapped whenever the talk veered towards Betty Longden's last night at Hadley House. It was a mainspring of fear that set Pearson's forearms and wrists and fingers visibly trembling. And it always happened when Mosley mentioned Kestrel Clough. Mosley had believed then that he still had time, that another night of solitude would do its own work on Pearson, with a great consequent saving of nervous energy. Now Mosley knew that time had run out on him.

He looked again at the Clough, stripping it of cameras, floodlights and microphone booms. There were fossils here that charted pre-human history. Men had unearthed here the bones of the sabre-toothed tiger and woolly rhinoceros. The crucial fault in the rock had happened before any man had set foot in these hills. And there was something else that had happened more recently, that was known only to the eyes of those who had perpetrated it. Jack Pearson? And Ted Hunter? While Matthew Longden pulled the strings – and Isaac Oldham, ignoring the whining of his dogs, made sure he knew nothing of it?

Was it all going to devolve into anti-climax? Would they be sweating and straining and rupturing themselves shifting a mountain of stone, only to retrieve a bundle of Betty Longden's old clothes?

Mosley thought not. Lottie Pearson would not have brought Teagle here for that. Teagle would not have come; he would not have been an easy man, even for Lottie to convince. It was not hard to see now how Lottie Pearson could have come by a lot of knowledge that could embarrass Matthew Longden. She was an intelligent woman, and not only might Longden sometimes have talked indiscreetly while he was under her spell, she had also been married to Jack Pearson. She had listened to his empty boastings when he was sober and to his surrealistic droolings when he was drunk. She had not just put two and two together: she had added together bits from two sources, to complete her sum.

In the meanwhile, Lottie Pearson was doing anything but well on the film-set. She was unable to give Teagle what he was asking of her. She was supposed to catch sudden sight of the dragon – who was not there – and that was to strike her palsied with fear. But her conception of fear looked like a combination of constipation and pop-eyed comicality.

'Cut!' Teagle shouted for the twenty-eighth time, and followed that with a service-burst of obscenity that stunned the prim, bucolic watchers on the hillside.

'All right, sweetheart. Try again. Take twenty-nine!'

Mosley slipped unobtrusively away from the group, back a short way towards the farm, then – apparently impervious to stings – through a nettle-bed that brought him up a never-trodden gulch behind and below the natural platform where the lascivious princess was becoming desperate about her own ineptitude.

'Move your head slowly, sweetheart. Catch sight of the dragon on my slow count of three. And then jump – one – two –'

She moved her head and saw, not a dragon, but Mosley's face, scowling hideously at her through a cleft in the rocks but a yard or two from her, where she had no reason to expect any face to be. She started. The foot on which she was partly supporting herself slipped and she sagged into the ropes that were holding her.

'Perfect!' Teagle shouted. 'I knew you could do it, darling!'

Mosley withdrew and spent a minute or two scanning the ranks of spectators. He could not see Betty Longden among them: it was hardly likely she would be. Nor would she have gone up to the House – at all costs she would want to avoid any confrontation with Longden. And there was no habitation between here and the House where she would want to call for old time's sake. Mosley made a guess, moved quietly between the cameras and the crowd, and followed the path up to the rusty gate that he had climbed the first time he had come down to talk to Isaac Oldham. He clumsily climbed it again.

A short way farther up, there was a side-track through the trees that led before long to a ledge which commanded a magnificent view of the valley below, and the hills beyond that, and beyond them the interlocking folds of valley after valley after valley, the panorama spreading like a stereoscopic map. It was the sort of spot, not much more than a half-hour's walk from the House, to which Betty Longden might well often have come for consolation during the least tolerable months of her marriage.

And she was here now, sitting on her folded cardigan, looking out across the vertebrae of England. She saw Mosley approach, and was so unstartled that she might have been expecting him. She moved herself to make room for him to sit beside her. At close quarters he was able to confirm the quick impression he had had as Lottie had driven them past the afternoon siege of Hadley Dale. The greying of her hair might have aged her, but the serenity that she had never wholly lost in the bad years had now come fully into its own. Moreover she had a fluency, an initiative in conversation that he had not known her to be capable of. In every way she struck him as a woman who had found herself.

'Well, thank goodness you're still king of the hills,' she said. 'You'll have a lot to ask me, and I've been telling myself since we set out, what a mercy it is you'll be asking the questions. There are things that would have come hard from a stranger. In fact, if Lottie hadn't assured me that you were still about, I don't think she could have persuaded me.'

'How did she find you?' Mosley asked. 'And why are you here?'

'She found me because a man was fickle,' she said.

And whatever she meant by it, it was totally without bitterness: a private joke, which she went on at once to explain.

'Dear devoted Ernest Weatherhead. We used to see so much of each other, you know, sometimes for two or three minutes at a time, when he was doing unpaid clerical work for my husband and I came into the room with beer and cheese for his supper. And he was so hopelessly in love with me – oh, I don't mean that he ever said so, or that he was untrue to his steady Margaret. It was all on the highest of possible planes. Totally suppressed, totally silent – though I'm sure my husband suspected. He would, of course. I didn't have to look at a man – even if a workman passed my kitchen window, he didn't think it was an accident. But by the time Ernest was ready to turn himself into my slave, I'd have thrown the moon over the sun. I'd decided to leave. That was almost as good as having gone. So I was even prepared to turn Ernest's two or three minutes into a naughty five or ten. I did it on purpose. Oh, a change had come over me, Mr Mosley.'

She turned to him and laughed. 'Is this likely to bore you? There's still enough of the old me left for me to want you to see the true picture.'

Mosley wanted nothing more than for her to go on talking.

He conveyed that with his own rugged version of serenity.

'When I left here, you know, it was not without some sort of wrench. I'm not as inhuman as that – I'd been here a long time. I said I'd like to get news, now and then, cuttings from papers – births, marriages, deaths, all the scandals – especially if any of the bigwigs ever came unstuck. So I entrusted that to Ernest, and never was there a more faithful correspondent. He was the only one who knew where to write to me. Never did I think that he would prove faithless.'

But she was still laughing about it.

'But then I reckoned without the day when Lottie Pearson would ever want to get my address out of him. I take it that Lottie has never needed to make a set at you, Mr Mosley?'

'Not so far,' he said, making himself sound a shade rueful, entering into her mood.

'She might, even yet. My advice is, make the most of it. I am sure that resistance would be a waste of your time, in the long run.'

And then, as if reading his mind, she added, 'You must think that I've grown into an awful person. Where's all that old respectability gone? Was this abandon trying all the while to get out?'

'Just tell me first why you're here,' he said.

'To give evidence – if what Lottie thinks is the truth. But, really, it's too horrible to think about . . .'

She shuddered – and there was nothing theatrical about that. It was a sudden change of mood, suggesting that behind all this gaiety there lay a seam of apprehension. It had been no light decision to come here. She was not sure yet that she had done the right thing. Lottie must have nagged her without respite.

'Shall I begin at the beginning? I should like to feel sure that you understand, Mr Mosley – that someone up here understands absolutely.'

'Take your time, Mrs Longden.'

She shuddered again – in a different way.

'That name! And yet the right way to begin is as Mrs Longden. Surprisingly enough, I can still remember how I came to be in love with him. I'm not just excusing myself for the sake of my pride. I know why I married him. He seemed so much my sort of person. Rectitude, reliability, integrity, a man who loved all the things, as the Prayer Book says, that are honourable and of good report. To live a lifetime with goodness, without strain. It was no easy thing, in this day and age, Mr Mosley, to find a partner from whom one's integrity was safe. Do I sound like a prig? Did the people of Bradburn think I was a prig? I was what I was, what I was brought up to be. I was comfortable that way, and it was an unexpected joy to find a husband who was even a step ahead of me in the things that I stood for.

'When did I find out what a flaming hypocrite he was? It's easy to look back and see danger signs that I missed. Even on our honeymoon I saw that he wanted everything the right way – and that the right way was his way. He would never have claimed in so many words that a man was the owner of his wife. But he would sulk for days, if that wasn't the way things were working out. There wasn't even elementary democracy in his conception of marriage, Mr Mosley.'

She looked at Mosley to see that he was with her. His solemnity said that he was.

'I had given up a comfortable independence. I had known that to make any marriage work, I would have to be flexible. I told myself there had to be some disappointments; I had to adjust. I suppose I even got some sort of pleasure out of the knowledge that I was making admirable sacrifices. But there was another thing. It did not really worry me until it began to be a bore. I discovered that in spite of his saintliness, he was absolutely obsessed by wrong-doing. I don't just mean that he read two or three crime books a week from the library. That could be anyone's escapism. He came across dubious practices in the course of his work. He never stopped talking about them. He seemed to delight in rooting them out: it seemed the real reason why he loved pulling columns of figures apart. I know that you, Mr Mosley, were never under any illusions about the way he treated poor Ernest. And there were other cases: more than one: tax fiddles by men who were moral beacons in the community. It wasn't at first that I realized that he wasn't beyond using his knowledge to serve ends of his own. Blackmail is a strong word – but it's the only word for the way he treated young Weatherhead, and there were others. There was an enquiry agent in Bradcaster, a man called Watts, a failed solicitor, or former solicitor, or something, who traded under a high-sounding multiple name. He called Matthew in as his tax consultant – and you can bet that Watts is going to come into this story again before it's finished.'

She went on to tell how Longden had first gone in to consult Percy Allnut, *Chymist*. There had been something amiss with his porridge one morning. He had had a book in the house about Victorian poisoners, and he asked her if she had happened to pick it up and read it. She thought it was one of his lumbering jokes when he then asked her if she was regularly doctoring his food. She did not know that it was a serious accusation until he started insisting on cooking his own breakfast. It reached a stage where he was going to all sorts of lengths not to leave her alone in the kitchen in the early morning. She began to wonder about his sanity. But she knew that it was useless expecting any medical man – especially the family GP – to take her seriously if she went for advice. It seemed to be only in his relationship with her that this irrational streak in him came out. As far as the rest of society was concerned, he remained the model of probity, tranquillity, decency – and ever welcome good sense. Then one morning he left the kitchen for the front door, hearing the post fall on the mat – and she caught sight of their fragile little egg-timer. She crushed the glass in her hand, concealing the injury she did herself, sieved the sand through her fingers into the pan. He grimly took a specimen to Allnut to be analysed.

After he had received Allnut's report, he never mentioned the incident again. He knew he had been proved in the wrong; he knew the trick she had played on him. And she for her part knew that he would never admit himself bested. It was moral cowardice on her part, she said, not to have it out with him – but by holding her peace she bought domestic peace of a kind. She knew what this kind of life was doing to her, but saw no way of breaking out of it.

Then came the move to Hadley Dale. He had made comfortable money – including, in their early days, some judicious exploitation of interest-free loans from her capital, which he had scrupulously repaid. He began to enthuse about their forthcoming country life as she had never known him enthuse about anything. He seemed to think that he was going to be God's gift to Hadley Dale. During this dream period, revelling in advance in the freedom of the hills, he treated her with courtesy and consideration – formal and over-conscious – but easier to live with than the alternative. He did not even seem to remember the sand in the porridge. Then he learned that Hadley House was vacant, and his life's ambition seemed about to fall into his hands. She resolved not to skimp anything to make him the sort of life he was craving.

But the truth declared itself during their first winter of isolation on the hillside. Her attempts to enter into the social life of the village became the subject of a new domestic fracas; not that the social life of Hadley Dale was worth falling out over. She was becoming more outspoken now when they quarrelled. She presented Longden with an analysis of his character, his delusions of majesty. Forced back to defend himself, he became more rigid than ever. She began to think of the detail of leaving him, but the obstacles seemed enormous. She was now physically weary, and it seemed a massive upheaval.

Then came the affair of the man in Marley's cafe. It was no accident that her dental appointments in Bradcaster coincided with Longden's weekly commitment to his old Rotary friends, useful miles away in a different direction. There was something paradisical about her weekly escape, even if it did mean sitting under the drill. Even the smelly, jolting, dirty bus was a way into a world that she had been beginning to forget. Stupid ordinary things about that world had become strangely attractive: like the sight of a pair of elderly pensioners, eating chips out of a paper; like a colourfully dressed Negress carrying a creamy white baby in a papoose. She had never been given to lying, but she had no qualms about stretching the truth about her dental commitments. And she met the man at the upstairs cafe table. She met him once – and then only because there was such a peak-hour crush that the waitress asked her if she would mind sharing.

He was some years younger than her. He was pleasant, well-spoken and interested in things that had not interested other men that she had met for some years: like Betjeman's poems and Lowry. They liked each other and talked – talked long after it was fair to keep other people waiting for places. They never saw each other again.

But sitting at another table were two or three women who had been to a convention of some Christian organization, one of whose particular concerns was the sanctity of marriage. They – or one of them – sent an anonymous letter to Longden. Longden employed a private eye – his wife believed it was Watts – to try to find out at the cafe who the man was. Whoever it was – and whatever was later told to Mosley – the agent produced a name: Martin Bleasdale. There was a furious and infuriating scene, in the course of which Longden dropped that name in front of Betty.

She continued her visits to Bradcaster: fortunately there were two or three genuine appointments still on her card. She made Marley's an inviolable habit, partly in the hope of meeting Bleasdale again, but also now for the incipient tingle of rebellion.

Now she was doing something more than toy with dreams of leaving Matthew. It had begun with day-dreams, but they led her to the thought that it was up to her to realize them. It dawned on her that this could be more than an image dancing on eddying air. It could be made to materialize – if only she were not so dammed lazy about it. It was a prime example, she told Mosley, of what the scientists meant when they used the word *inertia*: a natural disinclination to disturb present conditions.

'Up to now,' she said, 'I'd stuck steadfastly to the marriage ceremony. Did I say just now that I was a prig? There are people to whom such things are solemn – and I was one of them. Until suddenly I saw a new angle of the God to whom I'd made my vows. If he was merciless enough to hold me to them in my set of circumstances then what the hell was Christianity all about? Could he really be harsher with me than he wanted me to be with my neighbour? I don't know whether that's sound theology, Mr Mosley – but I came out of it liberated. Call it what you will – playing with conscience, if you like. It worked, and when I had a second round of doubts, I pushed them

adamantly down again. I started planning in concrete terms –
and though I say it myself, pretty artfully.'

Did it seem real? Stretched in front of them lay the living
map, in an infinity of greens and browns, extending to a blue
blur of distant trees. Something had excited a congregation of
rooks nearer at hand, and they were wheeling about each other
in what seemed to be communal anger.

'Aren't they supposed to be holding judgement over one of
their flock when that happens?'

'That's what I've always believed,' Mosley said. 'And I
suppose at this stage your husband had been told that you were
still meeting Bleasdale?'

'He began to behave horribly. Of course, I can see that if he
really believed I was deceiving him, I could hardly expect placid
forgiveness. But I began to wonder whether it was turning his
mind. We had that terrible business about the car-wheels. In a
way, it was the gritty porridge all over again, but this was so
horribly worse. In the case of the porridge, I could say he was
making a mistake – an absurd one, a nasty one, an insulting one
to me – but still genuinely a misjudgement. But in the case of
the car-wheels, it was something he must have organized
himself, with the help of that irresponsible lout Pearson. It was
paranoia, and I was frightened. I flogged my brains for ways of
getting away more quickly than I was planning.'

'Stop a minute. Didn't he sack Pearson over loosening those
wheels?'

'He did. Or he appeared to. It was one thing one minute,
another the next. He'd say he knew for certain I was planning to
kill him. But it wouldn't have killed him. He'd not have got far
from the garage, with the wheels as loose as they were. I wanted
him out of the way so that I could use his life's earnings to set
myself up with this man. Then he'd have doubts, and say it was
Pearson who'd done it, trying to get even for having been ticked
off about something. To say that my head was spinning is the
understatement of this century. He said it all again and again.

'I was desperate to be away, to put distance between myself
and Hadley. I was never without funds, and I was hoping to buy
a property a few miles south-west of my childhood home. I had
a solicitor down there, pressing on with the deeds. But it all had

to be done with such secrecy. I was going to change my name. I thought I needed time to get myself a self-respecting job. But everything seemed held up until I was actually there, and there seemed so many things to do before I could go. You may think I was slow. I had got out of the habit of being anything else.'

She was not serene now. She was a trifle flushed, and it was obvious that behind her words the chaos of those days was re-creating itself.

'It was Ted Hunter who launched me. Tell me, is he in trouble? I'm not surprised. I don't suppose that in the last count anyone can help Ted Hunter. In the last count, he wouldn't let them. Ted Hunter was a mixed-up man, but speak as I find, in the time that he worked for us, I had no cause to complain. He liked me, or seemed to, and would do anything for me. And one day he called me over to the edge of the plantation – he was putting in a couple of hours one evening – and told me for God's sake to be out of the way next Tuesday. Whatever lies I had to tell, whatever I could manage to concoct, I mustn't be in Hadley House next Tuesday night. I asked him what he meant, got really shirty with him when he refused to be more explicit.

'I said if he was going to talk nonsense like this, I would call Matthew to come and see what it was about.

' "For Christ's sake don't do that, Mrs Longden. You'll have him in one of his rages."

' "Well, is it a job for the police, then?"

' "Oh, no – God Almighty! Keep them out of it!"

'I thought that perhaps we were going to be burgled. Perhaps Hunter had heard something. He was a man one believed to keep all kinds of company. And perhaps he did not want the police in, because he did not want his friends to be caught – or to think he'd betrayed them. Isn't it marvellous what you'll believe, when you don't want to face up to the truth? I thought of taking Matthew into my confidence. I don't know whether you'll believe me when I say that that just wasn't possible? He wasn't talking to me. We weren't eating together. I was getting what food I could when he was clear of the kitchen. That was the sort of situation we had got ourselves into. It was no sort of scene for trying to talk to him about a lunatic message from an odd-job man. I took the easy way out – or at least my brain did

141

– or whatever was doing relief duty for a brain. I decided to disbelieve the story.'

The rooks had settled down now, and in the distance they suddenly heard a cheer. Some herd triviality must have appealed to the crowd watching the filming. Perhaps Lottie had pulled off another scene to her producer's satisfaction.

'For the next day or two, and over the weekend, I did nothing. If I picked up the phone to make a booking at a hotel, Matthew was bound to hear the touch on the bell, and saunter into the room to see who I was contacting now. Then something happened that sent me scorching into action. On the Monday morning I came across Matthew in our all-purpose workshop-shed, cleaning a gun. Now shooting was one of the things he had always promised himself in the country, but it had never come to much. About the only time he had seriously gone out with a fire-arm was when we had an influx of rats round the sheds – and we'd no complaints on that score recently. I asked him as amiably as I could whether he thought we were going to be attacked, and he sullenly told me not to be childish. It was then I decided I was taking no chances. I would take Ted Hunter at his word. The bedlam that this home was becoming was sufficient for flight.

'I took a chance with the phone. I asked Ernest Weatherhead to meet me that evening at Crawdon in his car. To get there I lost myself at the end of an afternoon walk. I packed two suit-cases and hid them in an under-sink cupboard. I wrote a note to Hunter asking him to get those for me. He never did. I don't know whether he ever got my message. It cost me a fortune in new outfits and that was the most satisfying spending spree I ever went on. I think that you know all the rest –'

'Do I?'

'Did you never cotton on that it was Ernest who went through with that business of the airline tickets in the call-box?'

'I didn't know he was doing it under your orders.'

'It was my own, my entire idea. I am proud of it to this day. Though I doubted whether Ernest would have the nerve to carry it off.'

'He did. And he stayed loyal to you. I think I would actually have had to produce a charge of murder before he'd have admitted that it was for you that he did it.'

'God bless him.'

'But one of the private eyes, you know, that your husband employed, a Scot called Houston, was convinced you had gone off on the London train. He had even been loaned a photograph – of some other woman – who really and truly was on Bradcaster station.'

The blood came into her face again.

'I didn't know that. But there's the proof, don't you see? He had a photograph of some other woman. He was clearly in league with that woman. I can't help thinking – it's my nasty mind – it's the sort of arrangement he'd have Watts put in hand for him. Watts wouldn't know what it was about. There was no reason for him to suspect he was covering a murder. But it was going to be murder, wasn't it, Mr Mosley, if I'd stayed in Hadley that Monday night? The woman on the London train was to be proof that I was still alive. Lottie will dance a fandango when she hears this. She'd worked out such a lot, but not that – a fantastic woman. She had her knife in Matthew's ribs, and she was twisting and twisting.'

'But the woman on the plane to Amsterdam superseded everything else. Thanks to her, Matthew Longden was cleared – and Jack Pearson and Ted Hunter, and anyone else who might have helped them –'

'For the time being. Until he started treating Lottie Pearson the way he had treated me.'

'So tonight,' Mosley said, 'we are going to be treated to a sight from which brave men will want to turn their eyes. A disinterment – of your two old suit-cases?'

Betty Longden looked away to the horizon before she replied.

'Let's hope it's a false alarm – however much face Lottie loses.'

'I'd better be moving,' Mosley said. 'There are one or two things that I ought to be doing.'

'And Lottie will be wondering what's happened to me.'

For the first part of their walk back to the Clough they did not talk much. Then Betty Longden started to prattle, as if inconsequentially.

'You're falling down on your detective's routines, Mr Mosley. You haven't asked me where I live, how I live, what my arrangements are, whether there's a man in the offing . . .'

Mosley gave no more than a grunt. It was possible that his brain was juggling with the night's dispositions.

'I have a lovely house, in a place where I've longed to be since I was a girl. I am chief receptionist at a busy group veterinary surgery. Oh, and there is a man in the case. It will solve various minor problems, when this dust has all settled, if we are in a position to marry in the orthodox way. He is already free.'

The crowd loosed off an ironic cheer, and as they came in sight of Teagle's arena, they saw that a knight in chrome-painted armour was standing with a hilariously buckled sword. The plot of the commercial – if plot is not too portentous a word – was that two knights were going to be in trouble after attacking the sleepy monitor with inferior metal. The flames from the cylinder and nozzle were going to melt the first blade and curl the second one up like macaroni in a casserole. Then along would come the true esquire, with a brand of the same tempered steel that went into the thinking man's brand of twentieth-century razor-blades. Still roped to her rock, Lottie Pearson was waiting with unlimited favours for her rescuers. She was having a good deal more success with her innuendoes of intimate generosity, than she had had with her panic.

Teagle, often faced with a budget, and with the problems of putting together an act at short notice, had had troubles in the past with the actors' union. He was notorious for the strokes of luck he had had with amateur talent. Brad Oldroyd had performed as knight number one. Tom Appleyard had followed him into the dragon's lair. But Joe Ormerod had proved difficult to direct in the role of the triumphant swashbuckler: when it came to translating emotions into nuances of reaction, he could not be called a natural. Teagle, his tones enriched by an amplified megaphone, as well as by the resonance of the Clough, said a few more words that were received in express-ionless silence by the inheritors of Hadley Dale's puritanism.

Then Teagle caught sight of Mosley.

'Can you spare a few minutes, Inspector?'

Mosley looked for a few seconds as if he were considering the pros and cons of it, then he plodded over to the production platform. It did not take him long to master the few simple charades that were asked of him.

When the last shot was on the video-tape, and the engineers had begun stowing their apparatus away with practised agility, Teagle turned to the crowd, and in his best Bugs Bunny manner announced, 'That's all folks.'

But Hadley Dale seemed reluctant to return to their hearths. It was almost as if no one believed that the entertainment was done. Some sightseers even climbed over the boulders to see from close quarters the rock to which Lottie had been tied, as if a lump of stone that had been with them all their lives had taken on some vital new entity.

But eventually the last stragglers in the column were disappearing down the hill towards Isaac Oldham's fences. Teagle came and stood at Mosley's side, surveying the now deserted scatter of rubble. Mosley had extended his arm, and was making strange and inexplicable movements with his fingers, as if he were conducting an orchestra.

'How many hundred tons of that do you suppose we shall have to shift?' Teagle asked him. 'And what do you suppose the technicians' union is going to say, when they learn they are going to do scab labour in stone-breakers' country? Is there anywhere near here where we can hire a mechanical digger?'

'Won't be necessary,' Mosley said. 'I happen to be reasonably well acquainted with the couple who disposed of what's down there, and they wouldn't have expended any energy that could be saved. They wouldn't have moved more than one or two rocks.'

He traced another arabesque in the air with his right arm, as if taking the range first of one fallen slab, then of another.

'It's rather like looking at the pattern of balls in a snooker game, and trying to work out how they lay before the last stroke.'

'A bit tough, I'd have thought,' Teagle said. 'It's seven years since it happened. You won't find many signs of what slid and what tumbled.'

'Oh, I don't know . . .'

It was true. There was nothing that struck the eye with immediate significance. If it were true that a sepulchre had been sealed, as it were, by the landslip of relatively few boulders then moss would have been torn away as they slithered. Lichens would have been scraped from rock-faces. Surfaces would have been chipped, and there would have been variegated colours where stone had been exposed. But moss and lichens had had more than time enough to replace themselves. Weather and blown dust had restored an uninformative uniformity to all surfaces.

'I'm going down to fetch Isaac,' Mosley said. 'He's lived here since he was a lad. He'd know if a pebble had shifted.'

Isaac did know. Some cynics might have thought that Isaac Oldham had never not known. But he went through the motions of examining the rubble from several angles, then scratching his head.

'I'd say, you know, that big bugger there – the one that's the shape of a ram's arse – that used to lie on its side. And the one that's half under it – that's come right down from the top. I reckon if you turned that right over, you'd find Tom Appleyard's name carved with a heart and an arrow. That's from the time when he was courting Brenda Pogson.'

Mosley made a last esoteric sweep of his arm.

'You'll just have to move six big stones,' he said. And he showed Teagle which ones. 'Whatever it is you're thinking of doing tonight – of course, I don't know anything about that, any more than you know what I've got on hand – whatever it is, I wouldn't start too soon, if I were you. They've a way of getting to know things in Hadley Dale. Shall we say a quarter past midnight?'

'As late as that?'

'Let them get well into their first sleep.'

'Synchronize watches, then?'

There was drama inherent in Teagle. His wrist swept to the winder of his watch as if it were under a close-up lens.

Mosley went back down to the village. He went to Joe Ormerod's house, and was behind uninformative doors for the whole of the evening.

'At least we'll have somebody else doing the digging for us

tonight, Joe. None of that hands and knees stuff scraping soil with our finger-nails.'

'Oh, aye?'

There were times when it was difficult to know whether Joe Ormerod had the faintest inkling of what was in the offing. At others, one wondered whether he did know, but just staunchly disbelieved it. But he never uttered a word of scepticism, never a syllable of complaint. And orders, in so far as they could be injected into him, and in so far as he ever understood them, were something that you knew he would carry out in the face of assault, battery, physical pain, darkness, storm or holocaust.

At the right hour, Mosley led him, not to Bottom Farm and the Clough, but up to Hadley House by the open way, the main drive and the front door. There was a single light burning in the house, a table-lamp in Longden's sitting-room – perhaps the conventional way of persuading a housebreaker that there was someone at home. Or it could have been a signal to help a man find his way home again. For Matthew Longden was not there. Mosley toured the outside of the house and peered in at several windows before jerking the bell-push. It was an ancient system, with wires that pulled actual bells, hanging on metal coils in the hallway. They echoed in empty spaces, calling forth no life other than a skidding of mice-feet on deserted linoleum.

'He knows,' Mosley told Ormerod. 'He'll be down there. He might hurt someone.'

He conducted Joe through the plantation at the back of the house, down the track that could lead them all the way to the Clough. But long before they reached the rusted gate, even before the track down which Mosley had gone this afternoon to find Betty Longden, he took a path to their right, over tree-roots, loose stones and an occasional glutinous puddle. He had insisted on sparing use of their torches ever since they had set out, but he now banned any use of them at all. Very soon he touched Joe's sleeve, to stop so that he could listen.

There were sounds in the night – a witless owl, some quadruped in the undergrowth, fur among leaves. But beyond this there was a more distant sequence of activity, that carried to them only intermittently round tree-trunks and contours. There were the ingredients of a hubbub, men's voices, the clank of metal, once a brief tumbling of scree. They had not gone many more yards when the rounding of a bend and the descent of a shallow dip showed them a diffused light, shining up from the next fold in the terrain before them. And the voice came up specially clearly now, a picturesque improvisation that could only have originated on Teagle's lips. Teagle was displeased with something unimaginative that a menial had just done.

A few tens of yards farther down the escarpment, they emerged into a clearing edged by an exposed scar – in effect the tapering edge of the upper end of the Clough. Free from tree-tops and overhanging branches, they now had the benefit of a moon that had thrown off lace-like edges of cloud. Ten seconds from now, they would be in a front-row, dress-circle seat from which to observe the labours of Teagle and his gang.

But they could not move down there directly, for away on their right hand, Matthew Longden was lying on the cliff-edge with an uninterrupted view of the spectacle. By his left side his stick was lying askew in the grass. His right hand was supporting the stock of a sporting gun, and his right elbow was positioned to give him control of bolt and trigger.

Mosley motioned Ormerod to follow him silently in an arc to their left, so that they could get to the other extremity of the scar without alerting Longden.

Teagle was working by generous floodlight. The lie of the stones suggested that it had been a much bigger job shifting them than Mosley had let him believe. There must have been a near-rebellion in the ranks of his labour-force. (In fact, they had stopped work to negotiate a bonus fairly early on in the operation.) But progress had been made. Two bashed-about but distinguishable suit-cases stood on a ledge apart, sequestered from incidental damage by the stone-shifters. And the main effort had clearly been directed down a deepish chasm that had now been opened up.

Mosley stared down tensely. It was a tricky business, raising a skeleton, even one that had been laid to rest fully clothed. Its connected ligaments were no longer in a state to do much of a holding job. Teagle called for a tarpaulin in which to roll up the cadaver.

And Mosley rolled over on his side, shouted brusquely to

Longden.

'Drop it, Matthew. What good can you do? Do you think you can kill twelve of them, with that thing at that range? There's not one man down there has the faintest notion what any of it is about.'

Papers in his wallet supported the obvious first belief that this must be the young man from Marley's cafe. His name was Martin Bleasdale. He was one of those tens of thousands who annually disappear without trace – a knowledgeable peripatetic consultant in those specialized regions of private banking and insurance that have to do with the capitalization of promising ventures. In the final clearance of consciences, Matthew Longden admitted that he had rung Bleasdale – not risked writing to him – falsely claiming to be Isaac Oldham, and asking him to call one evening to discuss the finance of diversification. But Bleasdale had not reached Bottom Farm. He had been waylaid by Pearson and Hunter – though it was Longden who was the actual killer. The other two were mere labourers. They both agreed, when the stage was reached where that was the only option, that Betty Longden would also have been in on the act, if she had not thought to get in touch with Ernest Weatherhead. Hunter seemed to think that his warning to her ought to exonerate him from the whole issue.

Tom Grimshaw and the ACC were watching television in desultory fashion when they saw two knights' swords devastated by the breath of a monster that looked as if it had escaped from Hammer Films. Then a third knight arrived and slaughtered the monster. Then he hacked rumbustiously at the bonds that held an extremely mature-looking Princess on the rocks. Then she was throwing herself at him with lascivious abandon, stultified by the fact that he could not get his visor open.

But in the last shot, he had got it open. His knightly service done, he was freshening himself up, standing at a wash-basin, looking into a mirror, and shaving himself with gallant but delicate sweeps of a four-foot blade set in a jewelled hilt.

A round, idiotic face looked out from under the shining chrome helmet.

'I always said that man was nothing but a clown,' the ACC said.

'I must confess that I sometimes wonder if he has missed his vocation.'

If you have enjoyed this mystery and would like to receive details of other Walker mysteries, please write to:

Mystery Editor
Walker & Company
720 Fifth Avenue
New York, New York 10019